PRAISE FOR LEANNE BETASAMOSAKE SIMPSON AND *THIS ACCIDENT OF BEING LOST*

FINALIST, ROGERS WRITERS' TRUST FICTION PRIZE
FINALIST, TRILLIUM BOOK AWARD
A GLOBE AND MAIL TOP 100 BOOK
A NATIONAL POST BEST 99 BOOK

"Playful, pissed off and ferociously funny, Leanne Simpson writes irresistible love stories in the jaws of genocide. A genius shape-shifter and defiant genre-detonator, there is quite simply no one like her."
— Naomi Klein, author of *This Changes Everything* and *The Shock Doctrine*

"Blending song and story, humour and truth, *This Accident of Being Lost* feels so intimate and so familiar. It is the story of our sisters, cousins, and friends. I love this book. Simpson is a master lyricist, captivating storyteller, and a true gift to us all."
— Katherena Vermette, author of *The Break*

"Leanne is a gifted writer who brings passion and commitment to her storytelling and who has demonstrated an uncommon ability to manage an impressive range of genres from traditional storytelling to critical analysis, from poetry to spoken word, from literary and social activism to songwriting. She is, in my opinion, one of the more articulate and engaged voices of her generation." — Thomas King, author of *Green Grass, Running Water* and *The Inconvenient Indian*

"A testament to the power of connection, *This Accident of Being Lost* is by turns poignant, funny, fiercely angry and deeply sad . . . remarkable." — *Toronto Star*

"Leanne Betasamosake Simpson is a poet who strides through multiple realms. In *This Accident of Being Lost*, she carries the reader along with her urgent, direct address . . . It is the uneasiness and emotional uncertainty of her characters that makes the book strangely addictive. I was stunned by Simpson's generosity in sharing these experiences and inviting us to be challenged and to be lost. I welcomed having my assumptions about urban Indigenous people upended, and this is accomplished with the nourishing humour, wisdom, and poetic, loose-limbed lines that have been sewn through the stories." — *Globe and Mail*

"A stunning collection of poetry, song, and short fiction. These short pieces are darkly humorous, elegantly constructed, and beautifully sorrowful . . . The stories are not bleak, and a wry sense of humor glimmers throughout, walking hand in hand with damaged humanity to create a gentleness that combats the sometimes grim subject matter . . . This is a truly creative and heartfelt work, thoroughly modern in tone and timbre." — *Publishers Weekly*, STARRED REVIEW

"[Leanne Betasamosake Simpson's] storytelling philosophy is full of humour, truth, beauty, and love – and is always political. Decolonizing moments live within every song and story found in *This Accident of Being Lost*." — *Arc Poetry Magazine*

"A powerful collection of short stories and songs . . . [Leanne Betasamosake Simpson] is quickly becoming known as one of the country's greatest storytellers. Unique in its fragmented and casual, yet lyrical and elegant language . . . *This Accident of Being Lost* forces readers to look at Canada differently." — *This Magazine*

"Simpson deftly moves through and combines Nishnaabeg stories, the realities of indigeneity, and fantastical spaces . . . this [is an] exceptionally affecting work." — *Muskrat Magazine*

"Equal parts community allegiance and political reclamation. The structure of [*This Accident of Being Lost*] breaks from colonial modes of storytelling that cement their own hierarchy across peoples."
— *Quill & Quire*

"This is groundbreaking and powerful . . . Simpson is an unapologetic resister of the colonial state, she creates a world where ordinary fears sit together with acts of defiance against racism and cultural fragmentation . . . one of Simpson's more significant contributions to Indigenous literature." — *Winnipeg Review*

THIS ACCIDENT OF BEING LOST

Also by the Author

Fiction

Noopiming: The Cure for White Ladies
Islands of Decolonial Love
The Gift Is in the Making

Non-Fiction

As We Have Always Done: Indigenous
Freedom through Radical Resistance
Dancing on Our Turtle's Back: Stories of
Nishnaabeg Re-Creation, Resurgence, and a New Emergence

Albums

f(l)ight
Islands of Decolonial Love

Anthologies

The Winter We Danced: Voices from the Past, the Future, and the
Idle No More Movement (Kino-nda-niimi Collective)
This Is an Honour Song: Twenty Years Since the Blockades
(edited with Kiera Ladner)
Lighting the Eighth Fire: The Liberation, Resurgence, and Protection
of Indigenous Nations

THIS
ACCIDENT
OF BEING
LOST

SONGS AND STORIES

LEANNE
BETASAMOSAKE SIMPSON

Published in Canada and in the USA in 2017 by House of Anansi Press Inc.
www.houseofanansi.com

24 23 22 21 20   7 8 9 10 11

Library and Archives Canada Cataloguing in Publication

Simpson, Leanne, 1971–, author
This accident of being lost : songs and stories / Leanne Betasamosake
Simpson.

Issued in print and electronic formats.
ISBN 978-1-4870-0292-3 (hardback).—ISBN 978-1-4870-0127-8 (paperback).—
ISBN 978-1-4870-0129-2 (epub).—ISBN 978-1-4870-0128-5 (mobi)

I. Title.

PS8637.I4865T45 2017   C813'.6   C2016-901823-7
C2016-901824-5

Library of Congress Control Number: 2016958924

Canada Council   Conseil des Arts
for the Arts   du Canada

ONTARIO ARTS COUNCIL
CONSEIL DES ARTS DE L'ONTARIO
an Ontario government agency
un organisme du gouvernement de l'Ontario

We acknowledge for their financial support of our publishing program the Canada
Council for the Arts, the Ontario Arts Council, and the Government of Canada.

Printed and bound in Canada

To Adikwag,
wish you were here.

CONTENTS

I.

rebellion is on her way

under your always light 3

Plight 5

to the oldest tree in the world 9

22.5 Minutes 11

song for dealers 19

Coffee 21

i am graffiti 25

Doing the Right Thing 27

caribou ghosts & untold stories 33

Brown Against Blue 35

II.

a witness on unkept-promise land

constellation 41

Seeing Through the End of the World 43

travel to me now 47

Akiden Boreal 49

this accident of being lost 55

Leaning In 57

A Few Good Reasons to Wear a Long Skirt 61

road salt 63

Big Water 65

how to steal a canoe 69

III.

stealing back red bodies

minomiinikeshii sings	73
Circles Upon Circles	75
these two	79
Unsubstantiated Health Benefits	81
Tidy Bun	85
Selfie	91
Pretending Fearless	95
Airplane Mode	99
there are two thieves in this tent frame	105
Situation Update	107
Acknowledgements	119
Notes	121
About the Author	125

I.

rebellion is on her way

"rebellion is our way"

after they stole you & you fought your way out, no one was going to fuck with you ever again. get your own gun. set your own net. shoot your own moose. get two husbands & a wife & make them all feel insane with good love. give birth to a nation in an inglorious way, crawling through feces & urine & dirt & the bloody underbelly of betrayal.

She says:
    "use scar-weapons to hold the land around them"

    "infect tiny bodies with the precious things they beat out of you"

    "remember: they are everything we could have been"

kwezens falls asleep cradling the body of a duck while he weaves stories from bobcats & chickens & luck.

maybe-kwezens steady-slices through whitefish, while gwiiwizens finally speaks.

they all aim & fire.

standing up straight against this rock, i catch your fugitive eyes. before i turn & lay my head down, i'm thinking of Her escaping through these spruce, walking across these rocks, walking over this moss. i'm thinking of Her escaping past stolen, walking across lost, walking over shame, holding fire in Her heart, like all her descendants so effortlessly do, under your always light.

Lucy, Kwe, and I walked through the neighbourhood last fall, when all the trees looked like the time Nanabush hid his Kokum in there — like the maples were being swallowed by flame-arms of red and orange. We marked each one with a spray-painted purple thunderbird so that when their leaves were gone we would know which ones were the sugar maples the following spring. Really we should be able to tell by looking at the bark and the way the branches hold themselves, but we're still too new at it. Kwe was so pregnant I made her stand back from the paint fumes. Lucy made a stencil so the thunderbird would look like a thunderbird and not the death mark the city puts on the trees when they are about to cut them down for safety reasons.

Now it's March, and we have thirty tin buckets, thirty new spigots, tobacco, a drill with two charged batteries, a three-eighths-of-an-inch drill bit, and thirty flyers. The neighbourhood we're going into mostly votes NDP or Liberal in provincial and federal elections, and they feel relief when they do. They have perennials instead of grass. They get organic, local vegetables delivered to their doors twice weekly, *in addition* to going to the farmers' market on Saturday. They're also trying to make our neighbourhood into an Ontario heritage designation; I think that mostly means you can't do renovations that make your house look like it isn't from the 1800s or rent your extra floors to the lower class.

We know how to do this so they'll be into it. Hand out the flyers first. Have a community meeting. Ask permission. Listen to their paternalistic bullshit and feedback. Let them have influence. Let them bask in the plight of the Native people so they can feel self-righteous. Make them feel better, and when reconciliation comes up at the next dinner party, they can hold us up as the solution and brag to their real friends about our plight. I proofread the flyer one more time because everyone knows white people hate typos.

Hello!

We are collecting sap from this Maple Tree from March 21–23.
We will be by to collect it once a day, and we will pick up the
bucket, lid and spigot on March 23. Thank you for your support
in our urban sugar-making adventure.

FWP Collective

The Fourth World Problems Collective is us three Nishnaabekwewag, plus baby Ninaatig, plus Sabe, but Lucy and Kwe don't know Sabe is here. I'm the only one that can see him and only sometimes.

We're meeting in my backyard to build a fire, smudge, and make some offerings before we begin. We've had several meetings about the forty-eight words on the flyer in order to get the proper balance of telling, not asking, while side-stepping suspicion. No one feels good about hiding the fact that we are Mississaugas and that this is us acting on our land, but no one wants to end up a dinner-party conversation either. I fought hard for the word "adventure" because it is such a signifier with these people. It makes them part of it; they can be part of the solution without doing anything. Their only job is to file the flyer on top of the fridge with the bills and the permission slips and forget about it. This is the perfect get-out-of-jail-free card. Feel liberal in all its glory. No need to call the cops or the city; it's sustainable. *Help the Indians and their plight.*

We debated framing this as performance art, well I debated framing this as performance art because white people love that and if it were the fall and this was Nuit Blanche we'd be NDN art heroes. We could probably even get a grant. But it's the spring and we actually don't want an audience; we just want to make syrup in my backyard without it being a goddamn ordeal.

Sabe texts to say he is running late. Lately he has been texting me more than showing up in person because he has other clients.

He rolls his eyes when I say I'm his client. Kwe is sitting on a white plastic lawn chair, breastfeeding baby Ninaatig into a sleep coma by lifting up her "Not Murdered, Not Missing" T-shirt. She is laughing, saying, "This is the least queer thing I do." I try to think of something smart to say, like that there's nothing in the NDN queer rulebook that says you can't have a baby or breastfeed, but she already knows that, so I just smile and nod. I'm thinking the curve of her breast is sacred and sexy as fuck. I'm thinking how much I miss prolactin. I'm wishing the gentleness Kwe has for Ninaatig, Lucy had for me.

Lucy is wearing my black leather motorcycle jacket, chain-smoking out of range of Ninaatig. The baby carrier is at her feet, ready to carry. They act tougher than they are. For NDNs the tougher we act, the purer our hearts are, because this strangulation is not set up for the sensitive and we have to protect the fuck out of ourselves. I wish they'd soften for me. I wish they'd drop it sometimes, and let me in. I wish they could feel my warmth in the way that would compel them to give it back. I wish loving Lucy wasn't so lonely.

I mumble some Anishinaabemowin and put my offering in the fire. I think this in english because I don't know how to say any of it: This is our sugar bush. It looks different because there are three streets and 150 houses and one thousand people living in it, but it is my sugar bush. It is our sugar bush. We are the only ones that are supposed to be here. Please help us.

I think: Maybe I should be more specific, because the magic of the spiritual world is never super clear to me. Obviously I need their help. I'm an endless, wandering pit of need. They must know that, but I also know it's important to ask. So what am I really asking for? Help remembering everything? Help remaining undetected? Help collecting the sap the next day and boiling it down for twelve hours in my backyard? Help dealing with the authorities? Help while I sit at the edge of Lucy?

I watch the flames as they disappear my tobacco and carry my thoughts to those that care. We each take our turn walking around the fire in the right direction, smudge the gear, and put it into our backpacks. But we are not done feeding this fire. Kwe takes off her ceremony skirt, the one that she sewed tobacco into the hem but sometimes resents being forced to wear, and puts it on the fire. Lucy pours one shot of whiskey into the fire for their Auntie who passed away three years ago. I smoke my pipe even though there is blood because I am powerful and beautiful and sacred and I always deserve to be reminded.

Then we carry the buckets and Ninaatig to the car. I have three pieces of maple sugar from last year in my pocket in case we need to distract Ninaatig from reality for a few minutes. In case we need quiet.

I think: If I get caught, hide my kids.

We drive the car around the corner to the first tree. It's darker and colder than I thought. I wish I wore my winter boots instead of my running shoes with plastic bread bags inside them to keep my feet dry. I set down my backpack on the packing snow and put a tiny pile of tobacco at the base of the tree. Kwe takes Ninaatig out of the carrier and sits nursing. I see salmon, eel, caribou, eagle, and crane circling our sugar bush at the end of the street. Lucy rubs their hand on her bark. Sabe kisses my forehead, steps back, and then disappears. I hesitate, and then I take out the drill. I hope this doesn't hurt.

to the oldest tree in the world

i'm worrying about
what you're drinking
you're worrying about
what i'm breathing

i like you
because you
never
talk
too loud

i breathe it out
you breathe it in

i like you
because you hold
this all together
with the parts i can't see

i breathe it in
you breathe it out

you: eleven times my age
me: draped in clouds of youth
i think i know what you've seen
i think we're the same
but it's not true
i don't know
i don't

i don't know how to say this
without embarrassing you
but i do know
i believe in saying things
i do know
i believe
in the telling

your wrinkled grey skin is gorgeous
&
i hope you don't know what's happening.

I am 10 minutes and a bottle of cheap wine away from falling in love with you, which means I already am in love with you and that this fact was discreetly caged in the space of the unspoken and the unwritten and the unsung. Being in love with someone you've never met and only text still falls in the realm of unhealthy even though everyone is doing it and whenever the odd person suggests critical thought we just all go back to loving strangers on the other side of our screens.

Eventually this will just be normal. Remember when you could get addicted to the internet? And now it's just normal. Still, I'd like to do a little test, a little experiment, shall we say, on how real this relationship actually is, since there is no physicality to it at all. Nearly everything we do is confined to probably no more than 500 characters, so theoretically you should be easy to quit, because theoretically you don't actually exist. I'm going to start by not thinking of you consistently for 45 minutes every day. Each week I am going to double that time, even though that sounds extremely ambitious right now, but math says doubling things gets things done fast and I need fast because probably I don't have enough time to just think and text you all day.

I set the egg timer — ok not the egg timer, the timer on my phone — for 45 minutes and I am not going to think about you or anything connected to you for 45 minutes. Go. Ok. So I should have made a list of things to think about before starting the timer. Maybe I should stop the timer and make the list. Maybe I should make the list as part of the 45 minutes. Ok. Ok. Think. I'm going to focus on each topic for 2 minutes so that's 12 topics I need, well, 12.5 but the 0.5 will be my end reward. Or part of my end reward.

Topic 1: Kate Middleton

I am so fucking glad I'm not Kate Middleton. Like even if for the sake of argument we just set aside the whole colonialism/settler colonialism denial delusion and just focus on the day-to-day meaninglessness of her life. Shake a hand here, attend a polo match there. Kiss a baby, watch a tennis match with a fake grin beside gross William who's in an ugly old man suit and is also wearing a fake grin. And then the nylons. Like how many pairs of nylons does she go through in a year? I'm making it a point to never ever wear nylons again. Except I think I might have worn them one time last year to a talk because it made me look way more dressed up than I actually was. Why is England obsessed with nylons? And fitted jackets and matching skirts? Why does she have to match so much? How come no one tells her you can overdo matching?

Topic 2: Getting Old

I think getting old is about doors closing, opportunities lost, and a series of things you do to trick yourself into thinking you are going to have fun, do something meaningful, or have a break in the tediousness of life. I should do something about that, like before it's too late.

Topic 3: Doing Something About That

Ok. So the thing about getting old is that you know by now you can't really do anything about it. You can't. You can try. You can read self-help books. You can go to therapy. You can jog, I mean run, or read books or spend all day shopping at the farmers' market and then make healthy meals or do hot yoga. But whatever you pick to do, eventually something will happen and you'll stop and it won't be a forever lifestyle change and you'll be back to drinking red wine before 10 a.m. and making kraft dinner for every meal because you're focused on your maybe-novel.

Topic 4: I Can't Think of a Topic Even Though There Are Lots of Topics Other Than You

I'm staring at a postcard with a painting of a moose. The moose is staring at me. On the left-hand side the moose's antlers are skyscrapers and on the right-hand side there are trees growing out of the tips. I don't really know what I am supposed to get out of this painting but I like it. I like it mostly because the moose is staring right at me. I have its undivided attention. I could easily have trees growing out of one side of my head and apartment buildings out of the other. Maybe they aren't apartment buildings? Maybe they are long marshmallows? Or ghosts? Or square pelicans without beaks?

Topic 5: Body Image

Good one! High five! I have to fake that I have a good body image around the kids because that's what good parents do. Love the body you are in. All bodies are beautiful. I don't have any imperfections, just a storied tapestry I call my beautiful body. That's not really how I feel. I hate my body like everyone else. For one thing I think I have unusually large shoulders because my mom said, "You have shoulders like a football player," but my sister says that's ridiculous and that after 35 years I should let that outlandish and untrue idea go. Mostly I hate my upper arms because they are old fat grandma arms. I apologize to all the grandmas out there reading this. It is 100 percent me, not you, and remember Tomson Highway likes that in a grandma even though not really because he is 100 percent gay. Ok, so I hate my arms. I also hate my stomach. I was under the impression my flat stomach with abs was coming back even after 2 humans had stretched everything to oblivion but that's really, really not true.

Let's pull up *People* magazine and click through the bikini section. I can tell who got plastic surgery after childbirth because they have alien belly buttons. You'll be able to tell too. Yeah. A LOT of things get stretched out and A LOT of things are not going to snap back in place. One of the most important things that gets stretched out and doesn't snap back is your nerves. I know you thought I was going to say cunt, because remember when that white lady from *Weeds* said sex after childbirth was like throwing a hot dog down a hallway, and everyone laughed so hard and I couldn't let it go? Also I say cunt because I just read a tweet that said vagina is latin for sword sheath and OBVIOUSLY it is.

Topic 6: My Friend Nick

I had a drink with my friend Nick last night on the Garnet patio even though it's not warm enough and we had to bring the chairs out ourselves. Also he had soda water, even though that's usually my move, because he is on the wagon. I had vodka in my soda water, but it still looks exactly like soda water so how can anyone even tell. He told me about this disaster date he went on. He met this woman online. Date #1: She reveals she hates campfires, like she doesn't even notice he's a Cree wearing a plaid shirt. Date #2: She burns him with the bar bill. Date #3 (WOAH...buds, what are you even doing on Date #3?? because Date #1 is a clear deal-breaker): She thinks making records is a waste of time, when all Nick does is make records, and after she says this, he shows her his killer record collection. So he dumps her by not returning any of her texts. Then he tells his best bud the story while drinking soda water on the Garnet patio and bam. She's sitting behind him and sends him a mean text because she heard everything.

Topic 7: Pink Pants

Pink Pants is awesome. In my mind, he deals in essential oils, and he mixes them up himself in his lab across the street from my house and his potions are better than whatever you can buy at the health food store. I know this because I am home all day looking out the window, and people come and people go exchanging things in brown paper bags. But I'm not around Pink Pants. He is more like a reality TV show that is in real time out my window every day. I like Pink Pants even though he is not always wearing the light pink jogging pants he was on the day I coined his name. Pink Pants is busy. Sometimes he ties the push mower to his bike and drives around on his lawn to cut the grass. Sometimes he puts on a show at dusk that is sort of a fusion between white layman's martial arts and Lady Gaga's dance troupe, and he karates around the lawn with LEDs on different parts of his body and sticks that he wings around. One time he tied the hose onto his bike and drove around the lawn and watered the grass, but then he got into trouble because it wasn't his day of the week to water the lawn and our hell-bent-on-rules neighbour went over to put a stop to the illegal lawn-watering. Pink Pants also walks different dogs a lot. I don't know where he gets all of these different dogs. Or where they go. One time he brought my cat Moonshadow home because he thought Moonshadow looked chilly.

Topic 8: Keeping Score

Ok. I'm going to think about you as much as possible for the next 2.5 minutes because I've done such a good job of not thinking of you for the past 13 minutes and 33 seconds and this is my little reward.

Topic 9: I've Never Not Once Gotten Along with People Named Rachel

Let's get to the bottom of this. The first Rachel I knew did the Mexican Hat Dance (which was wrong for a hundred reasons right off the bat) straight off the stage of the gymnasium at Singleton Public School, but at the time it was Singleton Pubic School because some high school kids stole the "l," and this was during morning kindergarten's rehearsal for the Thanksgiving assembly and Rachel was wearing overalls from marks & spencer or maybe I was wearing overalls, and if so, mine were mint green and homemade out of the scraps left over from when my mom made my dad a mint-green leisure suit.

Rachel was 5 years old with glasses and she was the kind of 5-year-old that had teachers for parents, which means she never made mistakes and she was not messy and she never used too much white glue or returned her library books late and she never got lice either.

Since Rachel never made mistakes, her trip off the stage during the rehearsal was re-cast by herself as a fainting episode, which yielded pain-in-the-ass rest periods from Mrs. Pratt, the kindergarten teacher, a trip to Dr. Cupboard, and wheelbarrows full of sympathy from all the other adults.

Rachel needed a lot of sympathy.

And I apologize to all the Rachels that don't need even one little bit of sympathy.

Topic 10: Getting Old, Part 2

The only way to live a long life is to get old. I saw that on a bumper sticker. I really didn't peg myself for someone who was going to be so upset about the decline of my physical body. I never really liked my young body in the first place, and I never really cared that much about how it looked. I was more interested in what I could do with it. I think I wasted my youth. Like I should have enjoyed my body more when it was beautiful.

Topic 11: Being a Writer Sucks

Writing actually sucks. Like you're alone in your head for days on end, just wondering if you actually can die of loneliness, just wondering how healthy it is to make all this shit up, and just wondering if you did actually make this shit up, or if you just copied down your life or worse someone else's life, or maybe you're just feeding your delusions and neuroses and then advertising it to whoever reads your drivel.

Topic 12: Taxes

Good one, Kwe. Good one. You can go on and on and on about taxes. First you Canadians stole the land, then you make up this elaborate system of oppression to keep us too dead or too depressed to do much about it, then you create this elaborately irritating system for us all so that you have the cash to maintain the deadened depression and, admit it, Revenue Canada irritates the fuck out of you guys too, it's like our first point of agreement, and then, to add salt to our wounds, you make us figure out how much zhoon we gotta pay for the oppression. Don't even talk to me about roads and hospitals because we all know the irritating shit like the *Indian Act*, stolen land, pipelines and jails and nuclear waste outweighs the useful shit, and to add even more salt to our wounds — EVEN MORE — you create this undecipherable set of quasi-enforced and loosely interpreted rules printed on newsprint, which you get at the post office and that I use mostly to light big bonfires, while perpetuating the myth that I don't even pay taxes. Seriously, people, if we all stopped paying.

Topic 13: 45 Minutes Seems Too Long
and Here's a Great Reason Why

It's too long because time is different than it was before the internet. The internet makes time pass more slowly. For instance there is a radio station in Calgary that only plays half-songs now because you can't stand to hear an entire song start to finish. There is generally only one good part to most songs so let's save time and just play that. So that means, pre-internet, 45 minutes could mean 11 to 13 songs, and now it means 22 to 26 songs. So 22.5 minutes is the new 45 minutes. So I should really start with 22.5 minutes and that means reward time starts now, which means I can go back to thinking about you directly, and that wasn't actually so hard, plus I probably thought up some really good shit with all this not thinking about you.

song for dealers

she is standing on
tentative ice
glory singing

to a flock of smirking demons
sharpening their wit

to a choir of ten thousand cuts
widening their cavities

to blunt, tyrannizing wind
grinding her edges

to floundering normativity
unsure if she will bless

to the forming committees
pie-charting her reconstruction

"Oh love, come to me"
"Oh love, come to me"

I actually don't even know if you drink coffee. We've been friends, close friends I'd say, for more than eight months and I have no idea if you drink coffee. I think for sure, though, this is a healthy relationship. Like I don't worry about it obsessively. I have almost no anxiety around it. There's a normal, healthy ebb and flow. Sometimes you get busy with other things and with her, and sometimes I'm busy here too. And when I tell you bad things that happen to me you say nice things back and ask questions and make sure I'm ok. And you check in. Like not in a weird obsessive way, but in a "Hey, how are you" way. Mostly I tell you how I am.

Sometimes I seriously want to know more stuff about you. Like, are you a vegetarian? Or do you have siblings? Or which parent is Innu and which parent is white? Or why is nobody writing about class when in one generation there is going to be a massive shift from lower to middle class for Natives? Or does she know you text me forty times a day? Is that ok?

We're meeting for the first time tomorrow. Holy fuck. I just realized that and now I'm nervous.

I don't think you're a robot. Robots are what me and my sisters call "emotionally unavailable people." Well we just learned that term from reading the "Twenty-Six Things About Emotionally Unavailable People" on Buzzfeed. I notice with robots that they are actually better at typing emotions than feeling emotions or talking about them. So I like that. It is easier to connect with robots emotionally via text. I always wonder if robots feel emotions and can't express them or if they don't feel them at all. At the beginning of all my robot relationships I assume they feel emotions and can't express them, and just before I leave I decide they don't feel emotions at all because it is way easier to leave that way. And if you are going to leave, why not make it easy? I've never been wrong in this particular type of situation. So my point here is that I don't think you're a robot.

I do generally find robots sexy, to be honest. They can't connect emotionally so they are kind of depressed all the time, which leads to sarcasm, self-deprecation, and satire, and I like that in a person. A lot. But anyway, I don't think you're a robot.

I think you are healthier than me because you are very good at emotionally supporting me via text. I generally know that I am terrible at emotional support so I have a list of things to say when someone is feeling bad. I know from reading attachment-parenting books that you are supposed to mirror the emotions or reflect that level of emotional intensity back. Unless it is an unhealthy level — then you are just supposed to be calm. I always say, "So sorry," because I like when someone says that to me, although I can only think of one time that's ever happened.

This seems to occur naturally for you. I've never met anyone like that before. I also think you are a good judge of people. Like when I go on tour and meet fans — particularly on the east coast, because that is the only place I have fans — I say, "Hey, so-and-so seems really cool. We had a few drinks." And you are always like, "So-and-so is not cool. They just want something from you. What did you give and what did you get back?" Which is a really smart question because every single time you say that, I can't think of anything I got back. And then you type this paragraph that says friends have your back no matter what, and that friendships are reciprocal and each person gives the same amount of kindness, honesty, and commitment. And that friends are supposed to be there and that they give back and that if they don't give back then you shouldn't be friends with them. "Proportionality," you call it.

That really makes so much sense. It seems like a dream come true! Like woah! Imagine?! Like when I was a kid I had a stuffed Owl from Winnie the Pooh and he was always there for me no matter what happened. He was fucking on my side like no one else I have ever met. I have him still. I sleep with him a lot. Because having someone who has your back is important.

Every single time I've been worried that you are mad at me, I text you, "I think you are mad at me," and you text back, "Got you."

I googled "got you" to make sure it means "I have your back no matter what" and according to the Urban Dictionary it does. You suggest I write it down on a sticky note and place it around the house. I do. It's cool. Everywhere I go when I'm not on my computer I see this reminder that you've got me.

I'm in a bar telling Kwe that I'm meeting you tomorrow and she says I should be nervous. Very nervous, she says. She google-imaged you and says that she can't believe I've known you for eight months and that I have not google-imaged you yet and that you are fucking insanely good looking. She says I am going to be immediately attracted to you and this is a problem because I am already emotionally attached to you. I need a fucking plan. She says, in kind of a bossy way, that I should masturbate three times before I meet you, preferably once at the coffee shop before you get there. I am not to drink anything other than sparkly water or coffee. I do not want to fuck up this possibly healthy relationship with a drunken make-out session. For fuck's sake.

Holy fuck she is so right.

I decide to tell you I'm nervous because I've read using your words is key to healthy relationships. I type in, "I'm nervous to see you tomorrow because we've never seen each other in person."

You reply, "It's fine. We can sit at separate tables and text if we don't work in real life. Ha."

God that makes me feel a lot better. Because we totally could. I don't think I told you that I have social anxiety issues. I type in, "I think I might have social anxiety issues."

You reply, "Haha. I got you, remember?"

Good. High five. That was the perfect text, really. Like I alerted you to my insecurity around social contact and it also got framed in a potentially sarcastic way which saves face because probably I am supposed to be confident and sure of myself by now. At this point in my life I should have that shit under control. Now it looks like I'm funny instead of neurotic.

Fuck. What if I am attracted to you?

I think I really am emotionally attached to you even though it occurred over text. Like you know every single thing that happened to me over the past eight months right when it happened because, like me, you were alone in a basement apartment in a suburban deathscape writing a maybe-novel.

I wonder if you eat healthy. Like I used to eat healthy when I tried, and now I'm beat down and I don't try and mostly I feel bad about not eating healthy.

If I am attracted to you it will be fine because at the most we are only spending four hours together face to face this year and distance/time/text should take care of the rest. Plus even stunningly good-looking people have at least one bad feature and I am excellent at finding that and focusing on it and that takes care of the attraction on its own.

It's all good. It's going to be good. Trust this. You've got me. I write that down fifty-five times in my moleskine and then I rip out the page and tear it up and put it in the garbage in case tomorrow the book falls out of my bag and opens onto that page and you see it.

i am graffiti

i am writing to tell you
that yes indeed
we have noticed
you have a new big pink eraser
we are well aware
you are trying to use it.
erasing Indians is a good idea
of course
the bleeding-heart liberals
and communists
can stop feeling bad
for the stealing
& raping
& murdering
& we can all move on
we can be reconciled
except, i am graffiti.
except, mistakes were made.
she painted three white Xs
on the wall of the grocery store.
one. two. three.
then they were erased.
except, i am graffiti.
except, mistakes were made.
the Xs were made out of milk
because they took our food.
one. two. three.
then we were erased.
except, i am graffiti.
except, mistakes were made.

we are the singing remnants
left over after
the bomb went off in slow motion
over a century instead of a fractionated second
it's too much to process, so we make things instead
we are the singing remnants
left over after
the costumes have been made
collected up
put in a plastic bag, full of intentions
for another time
another project.
except, i am graffiti.
mistakes were made.

There is a hierarchy of people gun owners hate: Indians, vegetarians, "people from the city," and all political parties other than the Conservatives. My plan was to pretend I was a nurse of *i-talian* ancestry, but in the first five minutes of the firearms safety course, when we went around the classroom to share why we were here, I said in my most uncompromising voice it was so I could exercise my treaty rights. Then I applied my best don't-fuck-with-me face as the other students' necks snapped around to see the Indian-squaw-lady in gun class.

The older instructor is a combination of Lawrence Welk and Red Fisher. He is a blue-blooded Harper Conservative and he knows guns like I know I-don't-know-what [?] because frankly I don't know any single thing that well. He knows ballistics because he is an expert witness in the court system. He knows all the stupid mistakes you can possibly make with a firearm because he has been teaching this course for five hundred years. He knows how to hunt in a line like a white man because he is a living, breathing stereotype of the white man. He knows every gun on the market and how to repair or not repair them because he works at the gun store in Peterborough. He is Police Pistol Combat certified and Range Officer certified, and he is also a slug-gun specialist. His bio on the firearms training course website indicates his nickname is "Big Chief."

I can see that I could learn something from him. He is all for "girls in gun class" because the "ladies" and kids are the future of the *sport*. The election is in full swing, but he is not going to talk politics, except he is by nature a Conservative election ad and this class, in the finished, poorly lit basement of his house, which he refers to as "the ranch," is like every set the Conservatives use for their ads. It's impossible for him to not talk politics, so he keeps saying, "But this class isn't about politics . . ." after he says, "There's only one party that is interested in protecting your firearms rights." Just so we're clear. The only time he breaks from the Conservative platform is on climate change — it's real, he sees it, and we have to fix it. "It's reality. I've seen it with my own eyes. It's no one's fault." He raises his voice when he says "no," drops it when he says "one's," and then raises it again when he says "fault." Then he stares at us. The tension in his face whispers to me what he's afraid of: being misunderstood and having his right to hunt taken away by city people. And what he is not afraid of: hurting me.

Big Chief leads with a story about him and his best friend, Rooster, hunting in a farmer's field years ago. Rooster doesn't check that he is shooting the correct target before he fires and kills one of the farmer's hens. They do the right thing and knock on the farmer's door and 'fess up. They do the right thing and go and buy another chicken from another farmer to replace the one they killed. But they buy a laying hen instead of a meat chicken, and that's way more expensive, so they get burned. Big Chief wanted to give Rooster a "tune-up" for not knowing the difference between a laying hen and a meat chicken, but he didn't. The moral of the story is that you have to respect the people whose land you are hunting on.

My territory is zero minutes from the sliding glass patio door hellhole I'm trapped in.

Sabe came with me even though I didn't ask him to. He was waiting for me in the parking lot when I parked my firefly of a rental car in between the Dodge Rams and the F150s with pink-like-only-white-men-are truck nuts hanging from their trailer hitches. I know Sabe doesn't want me to go in. He's going to try and tell me to wait until the course is offered on the rez or do it in the north or do it anywhere but here. He is trying to tell me this is unsafe. I tell him he is being classist. That these people are no more racist than the soccer parents or the profs at the university or the running club that limps by my house every evening in matching outfits and then ends up eating cupcakes at the local coffee roaster's. I tell him I know my way around this scene, that while on the surface this looks like *Deliverance*, rural people are actually more kind and considerate than white people from the city. They don't pretend they like or get Natives, and if I stay within the confines of firearms safety, the thing we have in common, it will go fine.

The younger instructor, Eric, is clean-cut like he is the front man of a Christian rock band, and I'm fascinated by him because he is a little bit scared of me but he is not letting that stop him. If there was an apocalypse and I was trapped with these people forever and I had to pick someone to fuck, I'd probably pick him but I'd have to be drunk. He is making eye contact, taking inventory of which jokes I laugh at, and trying to signal to me that he is an ally by bringing up his recent hunting trip to Cree territory when he met "the Crees" and they didn't conform to his stereotypes, meaning they weren't drunk and dumb and shooting everything in sight. That's not why I'm fascinated by him. That's why he irritates me. He is fascinating to me because he is a bro-whisperer. He is skilled at the complexities of the bro-code and how to bro-talk around them, primarily because he is one, but he is also trying to manipulate them into a kinder, gentler patriarchy:

"If you know what you're doing and you practise, you don't have to brag."

"You're not a man if you can beat someone up that's smaller than you, like a girl or a kid."

"City slickers think you're a big, dumb, drunk, violent hick, don't play into their stereotype."

"I like a beer as much as the next guy, but don't drink and shoot. It's not cool, it's stupid."

He says it's ok if the Crees shoot sitting ducks on the water because bread costs ten dollars *up there*, and they are hunting for food and not for sport. Well thank god, no one wants to be a bad sport.

The younger one senses my suspicion. He wants me to recognize him as the good cop. I wonder why he thinks he can insult my intelligence like that.

I wonder if my classmates are buying this. I know I'm not.

Eric is explaining tags to us and I'm not really listening because I don't need tags. Big Chief butts in that you can't just get your girlfriend a gun licence and a moose tag and then take her along for blow jobs and cooking and use her moose tag. That's unethical. That's cheating the system. If she has a tag, she has to have a gun and be out on the hunt or it's illegal. He doesn't actually say "blow jobs"; he says "hanky-panky," but everyone in the room knows he means blow jobs and fucking like hockey players. I smile as I imagine her blonde ponytail swing from side to side.

I write down "Johnson and the boys" in the margin of page twenty-seven of the RCMP's guide to firearms safety because I just learned it means "cock and balls."

I try not to feel humiliated, but humiliation is the only thing dripping from the heads of the eight bucks that are mounted on the wall of this fake-wood-panelled basement classroom.

Sabe is standing beside me with his fingers on my back vacuuming the shame out of me. "Settle down, Kwe," he whispers. I tell Sabe to stop touching me and then I immediately feel bad. I'm too stressed and armoured for touching. I know Sabe is trying to be nice to me but I'm angry and hurt and wounded.

I'm a bobcat that's been non-fatally shot with a .22 and I'm still being pursued. The last thing I want is a fucking massage.

Sabe should just wait at the edge of me. He should wait until I collapse and can't do this anymore. He should wait until they beat me. He needs to stay close to me even though I'm pushing him away. I hope he gets that. How could he not know this about me by now?

The instructor asks me to pick up the pump-action shotgun. Shotguns are the firearms of humiliation for the Mississaugas. They are the symbol of our defeat. Bison, Elk, Caribou, Moose... all gone or nearly gone from our territory. Our land is such a cesspool that we are only allowed to use slugs in shotguns to shoot deer, mostly in cornfields. The land is so destroyed by these white motherfuckers, there is simply not enough space left for the elegance of rifles. I hate shotguns. I hate squeezing the trigger. I hate the sound. I hate the spray. I hate the kick in the teeth.

I pick up the twelve-gauge. I make sure the safety is on and point the firearm in the safest direction, which for me is a different direction than it is for everyone else. I pump the action three times to unload. I observe the chamber. I verify the feeding path. I examine the bore. Big Chief tells me to load two shells into it. I check to make sure the writing on the shells matches the writing on the side of the barrel. I load.

I am holding a loaded shotgun, face to face with the epitome of a white man. In the past twenty-five hours he has erased all of my people from our land. He has said "Indians" are only good for shooting cormorants. He has said "Indians" twenty-seven times in two days. And here I am, one of "their" women. The only thing he thinks I'm good for is what I've been marketed to him for: deviant fucking.

I look him in the eye in a way that makes him feel unsafe, and wrong. Threatened. Like he has met his match. I do not look away.

And then I fugitive-smile at him, hold my fake gun-school shotgun in the cradle position, and demonstrate how to safely get through the pretend piece of fence sitting in the middle of his basement.

In another forty-five minutes, Sabe and I will be on the road, putting some distance between us and the ranch. I'll have the flimsy white sheet that says I passed and that I'm supposed to send to the RCMP in Miramichi City, the T-shirt I won for getting the highest mark in the class, and what is left of my dignity. Sabe has me, the bolt cutters, and the five pairs of testicles he's removed from the trailer hitches in the parking lot, ready to be mounted on his basement wall.

caribou ghosts & untold stories

we are always almost drowning
we are the best trained troops
that refuse to fight

we are hyped up on aesthetics
and tripped up
by real life

we don't have time to feel these feelings
so we file that for
another day

we don't have to plan for the win
because we always lose
anyway

caribou ghosts & untold stories
bad timing
& smashed hearts

train tracks six pack riff raff
deadening regret
a collection of old parts

we get these little gifts
of tremendous, unclouded
by past dues

we get these tiny moments
but there's never
enough glue

we'll tie ourselves together
with bungee cords
and luck

bring the fish,
the fire,
& the new knife

catharsis is still elusive
so we'll save that
for another day

meet me at the underpass
rebellion is
on her way.

Dedicated out of respect to the intelligence and commitment of Black Lives Matter Toronto for halting the Pride parade in 2016.

We decide to get up early and paddle over to the bay that has a tiny piece of land separating it from the rest of the lake. The first snow came last night, reflecting skylight back at us from the ground up and bringing respite. We're losing fast and we all know it. The eagles left last week. There is a denseness to the colour of the lake that matches the deadblue sky and the deficiency of certain neurotransmitters in my head. It never looks like this in the south because the angles are different; there's never scarcity. It's not bruised because there isn't enough purple. It's not grey because there is too much blue. It's just light leaving, and I'm not sure if I can survive.

I'm up too early and I feel like I'm going to die — no, I'm feeling like I *want* to die. I'm lunging into coffee and holding quiet too tightly until the caffeine kicks in. I'm colder than I should be and sadder than I should be, but this is something I want to do and he is someone I want to do it with and I don't want to waste it. And here I am wasting it, on the verge of wrecking it actually. Why can't it ever just be good, he asks.

One answer is because I'm straddling the eroding edge of pathos, feeling the hole inside me screaming, and my left foot is slipping. I'm excellent at mostly hiding this presence. I'm tightening the muscles on my inner thighs until they both scream, trying to drown out other kinds of pain. Some of that's a lie. I never teeter on the edge of things. I live there. I cheat on myself with Sad and she never abandons me. In a way that will sound awful to you, but not to me, she is the only one that loves me in the way I need to be loved. My constant lover Sad, as muted, dysmorphic entrapment.

Another answer is that he lives in his own muted, dysmorphic entrapment that is slightly different than mine.

I decide to close my eyes and focus on each stroke, while doing what therapy lady says to do in these situations: imagine yourself as a tiny baby crying. Pick the baby up. Cuddle it. Soothe it. Rub its back. Love it because no one did that for you when you were a baby. Remember, sometimes you can trick yourself into being temporarily good enough.

That's so goddamn stupid and I can't believe it sometimes works.

I want to stop the canoe and I want to get out on the rocks and I want him to hold me and hold me and hold me until the hole stops screaming, but I can't ever find that in someone. He'll pull away first and the abandon will make it worse so I don't ask. I bite the inside of my cheek instead and cry without evidence.

I'm thinking of you too, though. Don't think I'm *just* sad. Don't think it's you. I'm thinking of you and I know we're going to see each other soon, although it's unclear when. I remember what you said to me in that dream. It's worth it. Don't ever think it's not worth it. I know you love me; I just can't feel it, remember?

He's in the front of the canoe because there's always a hierarchy, but he's being careful of that and that makes me love him more, even though I can't feel it. I'm in the back, crocked steering and hiding. I'm matching my rhythm to his and this is the unearthly part of paddling — the synchronicity, the glide, the moment when together movement exceeds individual effort and it seems like you're floating on air and not water.

We're moving faster than I think; we've already been around the island, past the beaver house, and we're approaching the spot. He asked me where I wanted to go and I told him exactly what you told me and I didn't tell him why. He just listened like he was supposed to. I didn't know how to make sure that I would be the one who would meet you, so he thinks we're here to shoot ducks. He doesn't know I'm here for you. You're sure, right? You won't come if you're not sure. That's how it works, right?

He gets out on shore and takes the shotgun through the reeds to see if there are any zhiishiibag in the bay on the other side of the clearing. I wonder what he's thinking. We're in this moment that feels like a miracle, and I want to like it but all I can think about is the leaving and if I can survive. We're still awkward around each other in a way that friends are not, and I don't know how we're going to sit and wait for hours if it comes to that. We like each other too much and the like always sits between us, surrounded by the ten thousand reasons it's wrong.

I watch his back as he disappears and I wonder about the kind of love that exists before you really know someone. The kind that seems so pure but never lasts. The kind that is light, unencumbered by damage and issues and talking. Just I love you as you are right now in this breaking moment. If Sad could let go of my hand, my chest could open up a bit and I could let this fleeting love in and carry it and steal it away from reality and play it and replay it in my head until it was the most perfect, infallible love in the world. It never matters if it actually exists outside of my head. It's always better in my head.

That's when you walk out of the bush and down to the lake. You are so beautiful. You look up and see me in the canoe floating on manufactured struggle, fucking around with Sad, as if self-defeat is nobler than regular defeat. Your body stands sure in a way I've never been sure about anything. Brown against blue. I don't understand why you picked me.

I think:

Fuck, please don't do this. Don't make me pick.

You walk through the reeds and lower your head to drink from the lake, less than fifty feet away from me.

I think:

It's clear you are making me choose. Perfect you, unfixable me.

and

I hate you.

I step onto the shore. Pick up the rifle, load, aim, and fire anyway.
Someone falls.

He hears the shot.

He comes fast and he brings three things: fragility, wild eyes,
fear.

The sun is making the water and his brown eyes sparkle. Blood-
red light comes out of his chest and into mine, like I knew it would.
He presses his body into mine, and there are tears in his eyes and
I'm so fucking naïve, of course he saw it all along. He kisses me and
he doesn't stop.

When you are shot with an arrow you die from hemorrhaging.
When you die of a bullet wound, you die of shock.

I kneel down and kiss your fallen moose forehead. I close your
eyes and say the same words as my Ancestors, Chi'miigwech gii
miizhiyan bimaadiziwin. There are tears in my eyes and that's ok
where I come from because it was love, not hate. And then he comes
to me again and he brings three things: tobacco, a knife, and some
proud, just for me.

II.

a witness on unkept-promise land

constellation

luck + intent = a star-person moving in

light = the unanswered thoughts of great mysteries

mama = your first ocean

you're used to quiet words
& so am i
so i'll just whisper:

you're a treaty, a dish & a spoon
you're a prairie, a big river & the mouths of many rivers
you're a longhouse, a tiipi & a wiigwamin
you're corn, beans, squash & minomiin

you're a buffalo & a bear amongst turtles

without conditions = that time we all prayed for your heartbeat

home = the place where the healer lives

nine months = the shift from spirit into solid form

you're used to quiet words
& so am i
so i'll just whisper:

i'll stand at the foot of your lake
i'll wait in the grass while you take it too far
i'll give you the keys to all the canoes
i'll sing to you, until you sing back

i'll sing to you, until you sing back.

I remember the precise moment it happened. The floor of the tiipi was woven with fresh cedar boughs that didn't remind me of Christmas. The fire had matured. It was mid-afternoon and the sun was high and strong but the air was still cool. It was simple. It was nothing. We were sitting. We were all just sitting listening to your Kokum reminisce about her life as if she was flipping through a book — a casual observation here, an insight there. We were there on those cedar boughs, listening to her as her Nishnaabemowin seeped into our marrow. Then, for no reason, you leaned in towards the fire, an elbow on the boughs, your body stretched out. It was that simple. You were just you being you. They were just being them. It was effortless. Nobody normal would have even noticed. But I noticed.

It was the precise moment I fell in love with you.

It matters and it doesn't matter. It doesn't matter because it's not the kind of love that changes anything, except of course that it is love and so it changes everything, but just slightly and never forever. It requires a great deal of care, as all loves do, because we need to come out the other side of this love okay. When I think about this part, I resist thinking that it would be better if there was no love between us at all. Because it might be easier, but it wouldn't be better. It's never better.

If I had your undivided attention, even for five minutes, I would tell you to stop panicking. I would tell you that you have no idea how amazing freedom feels and that you should stop giving a fuck about all those things you are supposed to give a fuck about, even if it is just for five minutes. For one thing, you'd realize that ice storms always melt, eventually.

If I had ten minutes alone with you, I'd tell you that I love you. I'd tell you not to be scared, because it's the kind of love that doesn't want anything or need anything. It's the kind of love that just sits there and envelops whoever you are or whoever you want to be. It doesn't demand. It isn't a commodity. It doesn't threaten all the other people you love. It doesn't fuck up and it doesn't fuck things up. It's loyal. It's willing to feel hurt. It's willing to exist on shifting terms. It's willing to stay anyway. It doesn't want. It's just there. It's just there and good and given freely, sewing up the holes unassumingly because it's the only thing to do. There is so much space around it and the space shimmers.

All of this would scare you. I know it would. So part of us tasting this freedom, part of this gentle, stolen, savage love, is to just give it away without saying it. We just need to let it be lovely and giving and overwhelming in every single moment. We don't need to do anything, except to stay glad.

The malignancy coursing through my veins would also scare you. Even though I loved you like this before, and I'll love you like this after. Fuck it. The only way to exist outside of malignant right now is to lie about having it. And I didn't want to ever lie to you or fight about whose turn it is to do the dishes or how we are going to pay off the Visa or whom you drunkenly made out with. If you found solace in her skin then so be it. So you deserve to. I want that for you. I want you to feel the rush of someone new, even if it isn't me, even if it's a risk, because it's always a risk. I only ever wanted to be the one that knew. I only ever wanted that dance.

I want to explain this to you because I'm going to be gone and you're going to be mad at me for not telling you. You'll think I didn't trust you. You'll think I didn't give you the opportunity to love me, to stay, to grieve with me. You'll be hurt and angry instead of hurt and sad. You'll be hurt because I didn't give you the opportunity to say goodbye. You'll think I am selfish.

But this isn't how you and I work. We never work through things together. We never deal with the worst; we just come together and celebrate the very best. You'd say that we exist in a bubble, that it isn't real, that we aren't real, but you'd be wrong. We were truth and it wasn't sustainable. So we sustained it through distance and time and struggle and persistence, because we know how to do those things and we're damn good at them.

I imagine what it would be like to tell you. You'd listen. Ask official questions. Offer standard support. Check in. I'd make inappropriate jokes. You'd worry and ask more official questions. I'd deflect. You'd back off to give me space, and I'd need you to do the exact opposite. I'd need you to fall into me. You'd worry more, which would lead to more fake bureaucracy. I'd retreat into myself, abandoned. By you. By my body. By life. Then I'd be gone.

I'm mostly sure this is how it would go. I'd become one more thing for you to take care of and manage; you'd become one more thing I'd avoid. I didn't want this for us.

So I didn't tell you until now, until this letter, which has been delivered under circumstances that are inevitably going to cloud your reading of it, so much so, actually, that I think you're never going to understand what I mean, which is why I'm publishing it. I'm publishing it so your friends, my friends, strangers, whoever, will get it and possibly even explain it to you. I want them to say, "She loved you. Not you the circumstance, but you. All of you. The fucked-up parts. The not-fucked-up parts and everything in between. She knew the lists you kept in your head just for yourself. She didn't care about any of those things. It was a flawless love. She loved you and she didn't want to own you or cage you. She had your heart. She had your back. She just loved you in an endless way."

I know what you'll say because you'll be mad. Angry like you're being falsely accused and waiting in a line while someone berates you. You'll want to scream that it doesn't matter. It doesn't matter if I loved you or not, because in the end, at the end of everything, I'm gone, and you're abandoned and hurt and alone.

You're going to feel betrayed by me. Death is betrayal.

And you're right. I took you out of the equation. I decided. I didn't think about what you might have been brave enough to say to me. I didn't give you the chance because nothing you could have said would have made it better and knowing that you loved me, if indeed you did, would have only made my forced exit more painful. But then the last minutes came, and last minutes can change a person. I can't go through that final doorway without you, so I ask my wife to write this last part down and then I ask her to call you. When you ask your wife to call someone from your deathbed, she does so knowing that this person is neither a friend nor a colleague, and she does so because this is what seamless love does. She calls you. She explains to you from outside my room. I can see her pacing back and forth through the tiny window in the hospital-room door. I love her right now and I love you right now and my heart is on fire. She is explaining to the man I love that the woman they both love is dying, is nearly dead, that she's been sick for months. That she hid it. My wife is explaining to you that she knows you are hurt and betrayed and angry, but this will be the very last time you will speak to me. My wife is speaking to my lover and they are both wearing the same makizinan.

Miigoaaniwi comes into the room holding the phone. She hands it to me and kisses my forehead. She tells me she loves me, and then she turns and leaves. I hold the phone up to my ear but I don't say hello. I just listen to you breathing. For several minutes we just listen. We are making love for the last time, two thousand miles apart, just listening in our fragile, shimmering space.

travel to me now

the wind has worn my edges
the cold pricked away brittle skin
bones lying here in front of you
lost before they can begin

there's red on the ice of the lake
there's bruises that never heal
there's past collapsing on present
she took things i didn't know you could steal

i cried like the ocean
i fell into your arms
my house is burning
& i'm ignoring the alarms

sometimes it's ok to feel that way
you whisper

take the covers off your makizinan
stop counting the nickels & dimes
let me cry one more great lake
kiss my forehead a thousand times

build me a never-ending fire
play songs i've already heard
tell me stories about caribou & skateboards
fill my silence with pretty words

i'll let your warmth seep into my bones
i'll let your light strip away the dark
i'll let your spring suffocate my winter
i'll let you fill the holes in my bark

build me a never-ending fire
play songs i've already heard
tell me stories about caribou & skateboards
fill my silence with pretty words

there's nothing in this
that isn't love

The brochure for Akiden Boreal is cluttered with words, a pamphlet of the kind that has too much information and in a font demanding a reader's commitment. But we all read it anyway, and saved it, and passed it around to our friends who get what it's pushing and act nonchalant for those who don't. We hovered over it while it was passed from sweaty hand to sweaty hand, babysitting it until we could get it safely taped back onto the fridge, behind the magneted pile of shit we can't lose and have nowhere else to put.

Akiden means "vagina." Literally, I think it means "earth place" or "land place," though I'm not completely confident about the meaning of the "den" part of the word and there is no one left to ask. I think about that word a lot because I approach my vagina as a decolonizing project and because metaphors are excellent hiding places. The brochure says that you can't take any expectations into the Akiden. That whatever happens, happens. That this could be your first and only time in the natural world, and you just have to accept whatever experience you have. For some it's profoundly spiritual. For others it's just full-on traumatic, and still others feel nothing. The brochure says that learning takes place either way. That the teacher, the Akinomaaget, will teach whatever way it goes.

I've read and re-read the Akiden Boreal brochure every night for the past six months and so has Migizi. The words "last place of its kind" are seared into my heart. A combination of fear verging on horror mixes with fleeting placidity when I get to the "Tips for a Great Visit" section. I'm worried that I'll have a panic attack or some sort of a meltdown and fuck up my only chance in this place. The brochure warns in stilted legalese that there's a "sizable" percentage of people who visit the Akiden network and never recover. They spend the rest of their lives trying to get back in. This kind of desperation is a friend of mine and I know myself well enough to know that it is perhaps better not to play russian roulette with myself like this and with Migizi. I also know myself well enough to know I will.

When I asked Migizi to do this with me last year he said yes, seemingly without taking the time to feel the weight of "yes" on the decaying cartilage that barely holds life together. People do all kinds of shit in the Akiden network, and in the tiny moment he said yes, it was unclear what he was saying yes to, exactly.

The network was initially set up for ceremony, but when people thought about it, there are all kinds of things we can't do anymore and all kinds of those things can be thought of as ceremony — having a fire, sharing food, making love, even just sitting with things for a few hours.

I decided ahead of time not to ask Migizi questions about our visit to the network or about anything else that I didn't want answers to. And you should know that I'm not sorry. We are from people that have been forced to give up everything and we have this one opportunity to give something to ourselves and we're going to take it. We are fucking taking it. Even though occupation anxiety has worn our self-worth down to frayed wires. Even though there is risk. After all, everything we are afraid of has already happened.

The confirmation number for my reservation at Akiden Boreal is written on a slip of paper, scotch-taped to the fridge, behind the brochure that is also taped to the fridge, hidden in plain sight. It is for three hours on June 21. I also memorized the confirmation number because I was confident I'd lose the slip, and on the same day I scratched it into the right front bumper of my car in case of early-onset dementia. I'm not good at looking after important pieces of paper so I also wrote it on the eavestrough on the left side of the house, because houses and cars are harder to lose than paper and no one will think to look there.

The number is ten years old now, booked on the blind faith of youth, in hopes that I'd have enough of a credit rating to borrow the money to pay for the three hours. Blind faith rarely pays off, but this time it did, and I do. Barely. The bank says it will take me the rest of my life to pay off the loan, but it doesn't matter. No one gives a shit about owing money anymore.

I arrived a day early in accordance to the anxiety-management plan I made, as was suggested in the brochure. I booked a massage at the hotel, spent some time in the sauna and steam room, ate leafy green vegetables, did yoga and cardio, just like a white lady. I was still carrying a lot of frightened that the two of us will just be caught up in awkwardness and we won't be able to relax into this place. The brochure suggested taking anxiety meds, and most people do because this is a more controlled strategy than self-medicating with drugs and alcohol. I wanted to be the kind of person that could melt into this experience fully present. I wanted to be that kind of person, but I knew in my core I'm not. I'm the kind of person that actually needs to self-medicate in order to not fuck up important things.

Migizi and I met at the hotel bar that night for a few drinks and to reconnect before the visit. It was graceless at first for sure. But after the first bottle of wine I could see him breathing more easily. He stretched out his legs under the table and let them touch mine. My eye contact was less jolted. He seemed more confident as the night went on, and the silently voiced "you're not good enough," which marinates in the bones of my inner ear and pricks at my edges, was a little quieter.

Now it's 10 a.m. and we've each had two cups of coffee, one at the hotel and one in the waiting room at the security check-in. You have to arrive two hours before your scheduled appointment to make sure there is ample time for the scanning process. Last year some activists burnt down the Cerrado, a tropical savannah habitat in Brazil, by sneaking in an old-style flint. They wanted open access, which I want too. But in the process, they disappeared the last members of the tropical savannah choir.

I'm watching to see if Migizi is nervous too, but he is good at holding his cards close to his chest. He drank three shots of whiskey from a silver flask just outside the scanning room before we came in. I had two because I'm desperate to be able to feel this place. I tell myself our Ancestors would be ok with that; after all, we're going to be someone's Ancestors some day, and I'd want my grandchildren to do whatever they had to do to experience this. Compassion and empathy have to win at some point.

We clear security and wait in the holding room until the Watcher comes in to unlock the door to the site. She does so at exactly noon. I walk inside and am immediately hit with the smell of cedar. It's real cedar, not synthetic, and according to the brochure that means it comes with a feeling, not just a smell. The brochure says to be prepared for feelings and to let them wash over you like the warm waves of the ocean. This is the key to a good visit, the brochure insists.

I feel my body relaxing in spite of myself. The space seems immense even though I know my Ancestors would think this is ridiculous. The idea of finding the smallest amount of habitat that could sustain itself and then putting it in big glass jar without a lid. The glass dome. The edges.

I feel like crying. Actually I'm starting to cry and I know Migizi hates that and I hate that too and so I'm biting my lip but silent tears are falling all over my face anyway. Migizi licks the tears off my cheeks, takes my hand, and we walk to the centre of Akiden Boreal, where there is a circle of woven cedar, like our Ancestors might have done on the floor of a lodge. He opens his hand and he is holding two tiny dried red berries. I ask. He says they are from his Kobade, his great-grandmother, and they are called "raspberries." He says they are medicine and his family saved them for nearly one hundred years in case one of them ever got into Akiden Boreal. I ask him if they are hallucinogens. He says he thinks so. I'm becoming overwhelmed in the same way the brochure warned us and so I decide to eat one. We both do. Within minutes, I'm more relaxed and happier than

I've ever felt. I'm drowning in peacefulness and calm, and there is a knife of deep sadness being forcefully pulled out from deep in me.

Migizi reaches over and touches the skin on my lower back with just his fingertips. It feels like he's moving around the air very closest to my skin. I'm losing track of my body; the edges are dissolving and I'm a fugitive in a fragile vessel of feelings and smells and senses. My lungs draw in moist air to deeper reaches, my back is arching, my heart feels like it is floating out of my chest.

Then Migizi lies down on the cedar boughs, on his side, facing me. He puts his right hand on my cheek, and he kisses my lips. He's kissing my lips, and in doing so he is touching that part of me I've never shared with anyone, because I didn't know it was there. There is a yellow light around his body and I can feel it mixing with my light. Part of me is a pool of want. Part of me is a waterfall filling up that want almost faster than I can desire. At one point he stops and takes his clothes off, which he's never done before, because he's afraid I will see his self-hatred, the self-hatred we both share and pretend doesn't exist. And we're there, in the middle of Akiden Boreal. Naked. Embraced. Enmeshed. Crying. Convinced that being an Akiden addict for the rest of our lives is important, convinced that living as an addict, dying as an addict, is unconditionally worth it. Convinced that breaking all of our healthy connections to the city, the concrete and even the movement, for the chance to be here one more time before we die, is worth it. Because this is how our Ancestors would have wanted it.

this accident of being lost

listen for the hesitant beat
sit at the edge of the woods
shape shift around the defense
ban the word *should*

follow the bluebird
past the smoke & contraband
my frightened lower back
a witness on unkept-promise land

hide under mindimooyenh's skirt
wrap swamp tea around your chest
fill your empty with smoked meat
vomit this fucking mess

weave spruce into your fix
forget missed shots & mean boys
tie these seven pieces of heart
use whiskey as your decoy

play by the skin of old teeth
the ritual of giving thanks
laughing hearts & feeding fires
compasses & riverbanks

i'm just going to sit here past late
the stars don't care at what cost
you breathe while i whisper a song
"this accident of being lost"

Auntie told me to paddle down the river to Chi'Niibish. When I get to the lake, she said to turn west and paddle along the shore until I see the mist of Niagara Falls. As soon as I can see the mist, that's the spot to lean into the lake and cross. She said that's how those old Mississauga Nishnaabeg Ashkiwiwininiwag did it, hypnotic hard paddling, drowning out the screams of tired arms and aching shoulders, keeping the mist in sight, in the corner of their right eyes.

Now I'm sitting on the shore of the lake, thinking about you, at the spot where I'm supposed to be turning and crossing. I always forget how big the lake is. I always forget how blue the lake is, the clean wind picking up drops so I can breathe them in. I'm imagining you're here and we're talking about you and me and us, and things that matter. How we got here. Where we're going. What's to be done. My impulse is to push the conversation to somewhere it shouldn't go, somewhere it doesn't need to go, and I catch myself. I stay centred. I need to have just one conversation with you so I can write this. I just need to see your movements, your face, your response to the tiny moments of life most never even notice. I need to feel your beautiful boy-spirit rise as you lie down on the cedar boughs, lean in towards the fire and listen to your Kokum's quiet singing on Zhaawanoog land.

It can't just be lists of battles, speeches, failed marriages, and betrayals.

We can't be that different, you and me.
We sit in the same place.
Facing the same thing.
We can both boil it down to a single statement:

"They want all of the land."
We both see how it ends.

Auntie says we don't count our dead because it's like calling them back, so I'm more careful and I say it in a circle: Tkamse, my Taagaamose, it shines across, a burst of light, a tiny explosion in the sky, a crossing over. Tkamse, my Taagaamose, bizhiw gidoodem, my clan brother. Tkamse, my Taagaamose, our Zhaawanoog relative. Tkamse, my beautiful Taagaamose, eniigaanzijig.

This tiny moment: It was Binaakwe Giizis. The light was rich and gold. The leaves had turned and, like you, they were ready to let go. The river was low to the ground and moving cold. You already knew. You gave each of your weapons away: bravery to Ipperwash, honour to Oka, persistence to the Zhaawanoog, clarity to anyone who was willing to see. You stopped breathing the next day and our homelands were erased. You stopped breathing and a million Tkamses were born.

Zhaawan and Niibin were waiting for you at the stopping place near Deshkaan Ziibing. They were waiting so that you were not alone. They were waiting to wrap your bones in warmth the second you no longer had to be the warrior. They built a lodge around you and protected you, like you protected me. They used our sweet, sweet grass to smudge away hurt. They took turns holding you, like you were their child. They sung quiet songs near your earlobes. They massaged your muscles until you could let go and breathe full breaths. They used careful stiches to sew up old wounds. They recorded every word your lips spoke, and they sat with every tear. They waited while you made your final visits. When you were ready, Niibin took your hand, kissed your cheek, and led you to the canoe, which you paddled down the river to the west, crossing back over the sky, into a better world. When they lost sight of you, Niibin gave your bones to those old ones at Bkejwanong, because those ones still knew what to do.

And after you were gone, Zhaawan leaned in and sang the song that says, Thank you for giving me this life.

Miigwech my Tkamse,
we remember.

you can cut part of your skirt off if you need bandages, hair ties, j cloths, a sling, rope, fishing line, shoe laces, a belt, a sack, kleenex, toilet paper, ear plugs, a hat, a protest sign, a flag, a towel, a trail marker, snares, or dental floss. also, if someone loses their loin cloth, you can whip one up out of your skirt, & still have ample skirt left over.

if you are in a big hurry & you aren't wearing underwear and you want to have sex with someone, it could save time.

if you want to masturbate, but you are in public, you could use your skirt as a tent.

if you're on the lake in your canoe & you drop your paddles & you forgot your whistle & it's too far to reach the paddles, you could use your skirt as a sail to sail to shore.

if you are ice fishing & someone falls in the hole, you could use your skirt as a rescue rope to rescue them.

if some youth of the day steal the canadian flag from the flagpole outside the high school, they could fly your skirt until they buy a new flag.

if you need to attack a fort, you can get everyone together to play a fake a game of lacrosse with the shirts, and then when one of the skins "accidentally" throws the ball into the fort, & they open the gates to get it, you & all your skirted friends can take your knives & axes out from underneath your skirts & attack the fuck out of the british.

(tested and proven to work june 2, 1763, at fort michilimackinac.)

road salt

pacing the side of the highway
waiting for rhythm to break
sweating for one more hit
before i come out as a fake

dawn gets eaten by morning
one lick turns into three
aandeg just sits & surveys
i know she can't lie to me

road salt makes me twitch
& more comfortable in my skin
aandeg can love without trust
let's assume that means she's kin

licking the road is its own humiliation
just like hostages first trap themselves
aandeg's the bird on a wire
like i'm a deer on nobody's shelf

this is how to die in a war
they insist doesn't exist
aandeg never sees the whites of my eyes
unasked questions, unsurveyed cysts

the snow will drown without suffering
the road salt still managing dreadfear
aandeg hacking overhead
until we're mid-road again next year

dawn gets eaten by morning
one lick turns into three
aandeg just sits & surveys
i know she can't lie to me

I'm lying in bed with my legs entangled in Kwe's. My chest is against the precious thin skin on her back and my arms hold her warm brown. I'm imagining us lying in smoky calm on cedar boughs instead of in this damp on Oakwood Avenue. I wish I could fall asleep like this, with her so close, but I'm too nervous when nice happens; I get more anxious than normal. I'm shallow breathing at her atlas and I'm worrying that my breath is too moist on the back of her neck and that it feels gross for her, maybe so gross that it will wake her up. So I roll over and check my phone, just in case.

There are eight new notifications from Signal, all from Niibish. She just made me switch from imessage to threema to Signal because Edward Snowden tweeted that Signal is the safest texting app, mostly because the code is open source and has been independently verified. I wonder if she knows what "code" and "open source" mean, but if anyone can be trusted about these things my money's on Snowden. Also I have no idea why she cares about internet security, but she clearly does. I have to look at my iphone every four minutes so I don't miss anything because I can't get the sound notifications to work on this app even though I've googled it. To be honest, this isn't actually that big of a problem because I look at my beloved screen every four minutes, whether or not the sound notifications are on anyway. We all do and we all lie about it.

Niibish wants to know where I am, why I'm not up yet, why I'm not texting her back, and she'd like my opinion on the stories in the *Toronto Star* and *Vice* this morning about the flood. "ARE THEY GETTING IT?" is the second-last text. The last text is another "Where are you? ffs."

Niibish is mad at me for making her text me instead of doing things the old way and she's right and I promised it's just a tool and that we'll still do things the right way once this crisis is over. She typed in "PROMISE" in all caps like she was yelling. I texted back "of course," like she was insane for thinking otherwise. Kwe texts me "of course" when she wants me to think I'm insane for thinking otherwise too.

I get dressed, take the bus and then the subway to headquarters. Headquarters is high up, like Nishnaabeg Mount Olympus, so we can see Lake Ontario out of the window. Only I call it headquarters — really it's just a condo at Yonge and Dundas.

We call the lake Chi'Niibish, which means big water, and we share this brilliant peacemaker with the Mohawks. I call her Niibish for short and I'm the one that got her the iphone and taught her how to text. I look out the south-facing window of the condo and see her dense blue. She is full, too full, and she's tipsy from the birth control pills, the plastics, the sewage, and the contraband that washes into her no matter what. She is too full and overflowing and no one saw this coming like no one saw Calgary flooding, even though every single one of us should have.

Five days ago she spilled over the boardwalk and flooded the Power Plant and Queens Quay, and we all got into twitter fights about the waterfront. Six days ago, she crept over the Lakeshore and drank up Union Station, and we called New York City because remember the hurricane. We found new places to charge our devices. She smothered the beach. She bathed the train tracks and Oshawa carpooled. She's not angry even though she looks angry. She is full. She is full of sad. She wants us to see her, to see what we're doing to her, and change. That's the same thing that Kwe wants, so I know both the problem and the solution, and I know how much brave solutions like these require.

Niibish is just sitting and thinking and sporadically texting. They call it a crest, but not confidently because she should be receding by now. The math says receding and math is always confident, even when it's dead wrong. The weather is also confident when it is happening, and the predictors are being fed a string of variables in which they can only predict unpredictability. The public is not happy.

Niibish is reflecting and no one knows how long reflecting takes or what the outcome will be. She is wondering if this is enough for us to stay woke. She is wondering what will happen if she recedes — *Will they just build a big wall? Will they just breathe relief? Will they reflect on things?*

Should this be a Braxton Hicks warning or creation?

While she's sitting and thinking she's also talking to Binesiwag. Those guys, hey. Only around in the summer, bringing big rains and big thunder and sometimes careless lightning and the fog that lets them do the things that need to get done and no one else wants to do. There's the crucial decision, which is always the same no matter what the question: Do we make the crisis bigger or smaller or keep it just the same?

I'm getting the log ready just in case. I've gathered my crew together and we're meeting where the nude beach used to be at Hanlan's Point to practise holding our breath and diving. Everyone sat on a log during the last big flood, until we came up with a plan to create a new world. Muskrat got a handful of earth from the bottom of the lake like a rock star because everyone had already tried and failed. I breathed. Turtle shared her back, and we put her name on the place in return. We all danced a new world into reality. We made Turtle Island and it wasn't so bad for a while. For a while we all got lost in the beauty of things, and the intelligence of hopeless romantics won the day. We're not so confident in our making powers this time around though. Our false consciousness is large, our anxiety set to panic, our depression waiting just around the corner. We're in a mid-life crisis, out of shape and overcompensating because it's too late to change any of that. Beaver's doing push-ups on the soggy grass. Bear's doing power squats and bragging about his seven-minute workout app and the option of having a hippie with a whistle call out the next exercise. Muskrat is in his new wetsuit doing sit-ups, and not very good ones either. I'm wandering around the island instagramming pictures of big logs, deciding which one will be ours. And I'm texting Kwe, telling her that I love her, because she likes that, telling her to just stay in bed because I'll be back soon and we almost always survive.

how to steal a canoe

kwe is barefoot on the cement floor
singing to a warehouse
of stolen canoes

bruised bodies
dry skin
hurt ribs
dehydrated rage

akiwenzii says, "it's canoe jail"

the white skin of a tree is for slicing and feeling
& peeling & rolling & cutting & sewing
& pitching & floating & travelling

akiwenzii says, "oh you're so proud of your collection
of ndns. good job zhaaganash,
good job"

kwe is praying to those old ones by dipping her fingers
into a plastic bottle of water
& rubbing the drops on the spine of each canoe

soft words
wet fingers
wet backs

akiwenzii & kwe are looking each canoe in the eye
one whispers back, "take the young one and run"
kwe looks at akiwenzii

akiwenzii takes the sage over to the
security guard & teaches him how to
smudge the canoe bodies. fake cop is basking in guilt-free
importance.

kwe takes Her off the rack,
& onto her shoulders
she puts Her in the
flat bed and drives to Chemong

she pulls Her out into the middle of the lake
sinks Her with seven stones
just enough to
fill Her with lake &
suspend Her in wet

kwe sings the song
& She sings back

kwe sings the song
& She sings back

III.

stealing back red bodies

minomiinikeshii sings

you are here, because you're in my heart
you are here, because you're my witness
there are long rays of deepening sun
there is flat blue
lake wearing prairie
seed inseminating lake

if the stalk is floppy, we call it a poor erection

we're in my canoe
in my head you built our fire
in real life i fed it my way
i fell grains and tobacco to lake
the long rays of deepening sun
kiss each duck and goose before they leave

if the stalk is too wet, we call it a penis soaking in its favorite place

we abandoned shore
and meet the parts of me you don't know
minomiinikeshii dances
past what should have been
stalks lean in her wind
patience growing mounds of potential

minomiinikeshii sings, and the universe falls in love

the bugs are going to irritate you
you're a hunter
and there's nowhere to pace
you'll be too hot
the sun too deep
but here we are in spite
here we are, in the same canoe

we are so happy to be together

i hand you my .22
remind you not to shoot sideways
you are here, because you're in my heart
you are here, because you're my witness
there are long rays of deepening sun
we kiss the ducks and geese
and i knock the first grains into the boat.

minomiinikigiizis = the ricing moon
minomiinikigiizis = the last moon before it's illegal to be together

I imagine that she looks like a stalk of wild rice — thin, graceful, full of hope in a way that's calming, not grating. Her skin is dark and so are her nipples. Dark like she's breastfeeding because she is breastfeeding all of us. She has good bones. I mean her bones carry the rest of her and they believe in her. They angle out of her flannel plaid shirts and jeans in a way that makes her easy to photograph, if that is something that matters to you. She has long, straight, black hair but she doesn't need it. She'd stun us visually if it were short or if she was bald. Same with her glasses. You can just tell she's from a good family, the kind that is so strongly rooted in land that they're creating kids that don't get tripped up by screens and jobs and credentials. If she were here in this canoe, seeing me like this, I'd call her Minomiinikeshii, after the first Minomiinikeshii, the spirit of the rice, even though she is not from here.

We're loading the canoe back on the car on the side of the road. The paddles, life jackets, orange bucket, and blue tarp are on the pavement waiting too. It's a *very nice* fall day, the kind that makes white people happy, the kind they call "Indian summer." We're happy too. We're happy because the kids didn't fight the whole time, because there's rice in our blue tarp, because it's warm and sunny, and because we didn't have to try so hard.

If she were here, we'd find her a canoe for her and her kids. I'd drive hers and show her how. I'd worry she'd be too hot. The baby would be bored. Her older kid would sit in the bottom playing video games and talking about movies I've never seen. I want her to like this as much as I like when she takes down ducks.

You're tying the canoe ropes down like you always do when we're together and I'm loading the rest of the stuff into the car. When I'm alone, I tie the canoe down and load, and even though we both know you're better at it, the canoe never falls off the roof when I do it.

I see a couple approaching you, and I hang back and wait. I look out onto Ball Lake and disappear the cottages, the docks, the manufactured beaches and waterfront. I imagine just two people in a canoe, with un-fancy sticks from the bush, knocking rice into the boat. I imagine my arms circling, circles upon circles. I hear the grains hitting the bottom of the boat. I hear the wind. I see ducks and geese sitting and eating and smiling because they showed us this first and they remember. There is nothing more gentle than this — nothing is killed, nothing is pierced, nothing stolen, nothing is picked even. I sing the song the old one taught me, even though he can only remember the first two lines. It's the kind of song you could sing while running a marathon. It's repetitive and you'll get lost in the canter. I suppose that's why it is a ricing song. Actually, it's the only ricing song we have left.

You're still talking to the couple and I wonder what's taking so long. I know you hate idle chit-chat. Your people recount the weather report and the news as a way of connecting without adding a single interesting thought to their tell. It's boring as fuck for me and I wear noise-cancelling headphones in public so I can't hear it. The kids are already in the backseat, plugged into their ipods, lost in screen. I walk by and I hear, *I thought only the Indians did that.* The sun spotlights his camo jacket and ball cap, and her faded high-waist jeans, her perm, her tennis shoes, their pride at living rurally instead of in the city. I turn and say, "What makes you think I'm not an Indian?" and I keep walking, leaving him to deal with the aftermath.

I'm old enough to know this isn't about how I look and I'm glad she's not here. I'm glad I don't have to explain the cottagers who poison the rice. I'm glad I don't have to explain how to hunt geese over cottages. I'm glad I don't have to explain that this is a road allowance and that's why we are allowed to launch a canoe here. I'm glad I don't have to explain what my love is doing right now so I don't have to feel the weight of her pity. It matters where pity comes from and hers would come from kindness. She would feel the trauma of this for us without knowing how hard we tried. But that's not what I'd feel. I'd feel like a fuck-up. I'd feel humiliation.

What I want her to say is:

"*I didn't know it was so hard for you.*"

"*It's not your fault.*"

"*I get it*" *meaning* "*I get you.*"

This is the part I never want her to see and I know she is watching from the lake. This is the part that doesn't exist for her. Oh Minomiinikeshii, I'm sorry. We're sorry. We're sorry we let them destroy so much of your body. We're sorry we're trapped in a hurricane of guilt and shame. All you want is for us to love you anyway.

The most terrifying thing in the world is for her to see me here, in the ruins of my people, because what if she thinks, even for a second, that we're trying too hard with too little, that we are no longer.

I sit in the car and the kids ask what's taking Dada so long. I tell them what happened. The youngest one asks what an Indian is, and I struggle to explain, self-critiquing each word as it comes out. I'm sounding like a goddamn prof, not a real person. I'm explaining four hundred years to a seven-year-old like it's complex when it's simple. She asks, "Why didn't you just say we're Nishnaabeg? Why isn't Dada in the car yet?"

I unroll the window and hear, "Yeah, as a white settler . . ." and I roll it back up again.

I feel guilty because maybe I should be over there defending myself. Maybe I should be using my voice. Maybe this white man shouldn't be speaking this. Maybe if I write this down, he'll look like the one that's racist or maybe I'll look like the irresponsible one.

Who the fuck cares anyway, I think as my irritation rises into my neck. They won't change and we won't change and no amount of talking fixes that. They want a beach. We want rice beds. You can't have both. They want to win. We *need* to win. They'll still be white people if they don't have the kind of beach they want. Our kids won't be Mississauga if they can't ever do a single Mississauga thing.

There is a zoo-like overtone to everything we do, and actually this couple isn't that bad. They didn't call the cops. They didn't bring guns.

I lift my body over the stick shift and sit in the driver's seat. I start the car, turn it around and drive over to pick you up. You get in and we don't talk about it. The kids want ice cream and we know better than to make this the big deal it is for us, for them.

these two

two clandestine eagles find you in the front of this lineup, signing things & pretending nice, wearing professionalism like it's a halloween costume. the leading one drops in from behind you & the tip of her wing grazes the small of your back in an oval that's method & rhythm like it's all you'll ever have & she is not going to waste one fucking second of it. then the second one comes in on a sharper angle & tight circles your form starting at your roots, rising & then falling. her feathers are the wind on the hairs of your skin & she's flying conical spirals up past your head & then down again brushing your heels, the backs of your knees, the cracks on your lips, all the while the first one's wing is whispering to the skin of your lower back, while her beak is sucking the burning panic from the place you keep it hidden, behind the sorrow in your breast's bone.

We were standing in the parking garage off of Queen Street when I told you I loved you. I made you walk me there because it was past midnight and the parking guy looked sketchy and better safe than sorry. You said it back immediately without the analysis I usually require of those three words. We hugged. You let go at the normal time. You let go and I didn't. It felt too good like I was cheating life. Eventually we both let go. Took a step back to assess. We hugged some more. Then I left. Minomiinikeshii swirled around with a skirt made of rice stalks too happy like always.

Now I am sitting in my car trying to slow-drink kombucha even though I want to fast-drink komubucha because I'm nervous about the parking garage incident. I'm addicted to this shit like I'm a goddamn Amish-bearded soy-jerky-eating hipster. I was going to add the word "white" in that last sentence but that would make it redundant. Kombucha is sparkly and tastes good and has ninety kabillion live bacteria cultures in it and Russian communist scientists think it cures cancer! CURES CANCER PEOPLE. Even though I don't have cancer just anxiety and depression and whiplash and maybe an old concussion and probably PTSD if it can cure cancer it can for sure cure me. I should be easy compared to cancer.

It's been five minutes and you haven't texted the "so nice to see you" required for reassurance.

If I can have kombucha twice a day it makes me happier than I should be. That's eight dollars and I for sure can't afford it, but I've already discovered four a day is too much. I'm old enough to know boundaries are good. Boundaries are our friends. Fences make good neighbours or something like that. I also have to buy it from fundamentalist gay-hating Christians or drive to Toronto which is not so great. However Ansley recently gave me kombucha culture or motherlode (well it's not exactly called motherlode but mother something) because she is a hippie's hippie so now I can make my own. It is a disgusting blob in a jar in the fridge that looks like a dead baby and I don't go near it. The real problem is there's like eight steps and I'm only good at three-step things. Actually I hate things that take place in the kitchen for the most part, that's the real problem.

It's been eight minutes now. You need to text me back before you get to the subway and before I start driving or I'm going to be checking my phone on the 401 and for fuck's sake that's an illegal thing that is sort of dangerous.

Originally I had no idea kombucha was sparkly. Sparkly with a hint of sweetness from blueberries or maple! How fucking amazing is that shit?! It is guilt-free. No caffeine. No alcohol. No GMOs. No polychlorinated biphenyls or animal testing or child labour probably! It's or-fucking-ganic. Blueberries and maple syrup are both stolen Nishnaabeg things and sometimes stolen Nishnaabeg things are better than no Nishnaabeg things at all!! It's reconciliation! It's freedom in a jar! I'm kombucha-drunk and delusional. Which is good because I need a certain amount of delusional right now.

Nine minutes. I'm going to start driving at fifteen. Minomiinikeshii gets into the passenger seat by just pouring herself through the door. She does up her seat belt, plugs in her iphone full of death metal and punk and is looking at me wondering why the car isn't on.

It's disgustingly hot out today in the city in a way that makes everyone no longer care about how they look, as a basic mechanism for survival. I like it when Toronto gets pushed past what it can handle fashion-wise. I fit in better. The air is yellow-brown and it smells like exhaust; the sun is out and the light isn't right. I never remember hot days looking like this when I was a kid. I remember clear blue skies on disgustingly humid days. Now humidity and smog bring a yellowish dusk-like tinge to the mid-day. Now I try my best to not be anywhere near here for the entire summer and when I am, I am reminded of apocalyptic failure.

Twelve minutes. I should try and be more secure than this. I really should. It would be good for me. Minomiinikeshii has unplugged her iphone and is making a new playlist because apparently I need it.

I wonder how rapey the parking guy really is. I think not rapey at all. He is just the overnight parking garage guy and he just has opportunity and nothing else. He is no more rapey than the average guy. That still doesn't mean I should trust him or unlock the doors or sit here much longer or roll down my window more than a fraction when I have to hand him my ticket. This is the perfect place to disappear me. No one would even notice I was gone until morning. But then it doesn't really matter if anyone notices you're gone. It matters if you are born with a target on your back or not.

Fourteen minutes. It looks like this is turning into another opportunity to be brave.

I wish I had warm black coffee instead of this crap cold black coffee from eight hours ago. I could wean myself off of kombucha with coffee, which is backwards but addictions aren't logical. I wish the spirits didn't always get to pick the playlist. I wish my hole would close so that when someone offers me respite it could just feel good not like a drop in an empty bucket with no bottom. I'm lost, I'm afraid. A frayed rope tying down a leaky boat to the roof of a car on the road in the dark and it's snowing.

Then I hear a bleep, see a red dot in the corner of imessages, swipe a "so nice to see you. safe travels. XO" and start the ignition.

I finish the last maple and blueberry kombucha. Minomiinikeshii rolls her eyes moves the passenger seat as far back as it will go and presses play.

She probably shouldn't be the most irritating mom at ballet, but she is. She has sort of liberal politics — like she cares about the environment, breastfeeds, and homeschools. That's three more things that her and I have in common compared to the lawyer, the ER doctor, and the chiropractor. So I *should* like her. Just like I feel like I *should* like white-people artists, musicians, and yoga. Even though that's insane and also not even true at all.

Ivory is kind of a hippie. A rich hippie. I never ever talk to her, but she is one of those white people that just will not have that and no matter how much I give her my go-fuck-yourself face she doesn't see it and so I focus mostly on folding my arms in front of my chest in case she tries to give me an assault hug.

The first day she started homeschooling she made a beeline for me, because she knew I was also a homeschooler. She went on and on about conspiracy theories about schools that made very little sense to me and then told me about her curriculum, which was based on a scavenger hunt. The one man, an Asian man, beside us said: "Scavenger hunt?" and she said, "Yes. SCAVENGER HUNT. Do you have those where you're from? You HUNT AROUND for things on a list." He replied yes, that they had those in Toronto and that he was not hard of hearing. Then she continued to explain how life is a scavenger hunt and for example she had to renew her health card and this was also a scavenger hunt, going here, doing this, checking it off her list, running back over here, signing this.

I couldn't think of any words to say. Finally she left and started scavenger hunting on someone else.

Most times, Ivory is fluttering around the waiting room, putting the girls' hair into tidy buns. One Monday, she said the words "tidy bun" thirty-eight times in sixteen minutes. She asked me if I would like to learn how to do a tidy bun in case my kid grew her hair long like the other girls.

"Would you like to learn how to do a tidy bun in case your daughter ever grows her hair long?"

"No."

"She'll eventually want to look like the other girls, *unless she is a lesbian*." (She mouths the last part.)

"No."

"Do you already know how to do a tidy bun?"

"No, I've lived my life in a particularly deliberate way such that I'll never be in the position of having to know how to do a tidy bun."

"Don't be so sure."

Burn. She's sort of right. Like if my kid did grow her hair long and did want a tidy bun I would be in the bathroom right now on my phone googling youtube videos of tidy buns and doing my best. And yes, I would produce a go-fuck-yourself dykey mess of a bun and my kid would be embarrassed and Ivory would rush over and fix it, like the white saviour she is. This week alone I've already bathroom-googled "games white people play at birthday parties" (and then learned to leave out the "white people" part because white people think of them as just birthday parties), "how to tie a karate suit belt," and "offside in youth soccer."

I fake a phone call and leave to take it outside.

I hate ballet so much that I took to texting mean things about Ivory to Kwe in front of Ivory. Like the entire "tidy bun" interaction.

The next week Ivory brings a chick to ballet. She ordered eggs from the farm co-op, bought an incubator, and this was the first one that hatched. Since all the chicks from last year died, having been eaten by cats or fallen down heating vents, there is no mother so the chick has imprinted itself to her.

She is proudly attachment-parenting a chick. *Cheep. Cheep. Cheep.*

The chick follows her around as she puts all the girls' hair into tidy buns, undoing the buns the other moms have done if she doesn't feel the buns are tidy enough.

All the little ballerinas love the chick, including my ballerina. All the other moms love the chick because it is so cute.

Sooooooo cute! Oh. My. God. That is so CUTE! *Cheep. Cheep. Cheep.*

I feel bad for this chick. It's in an impossible situation. Imprinted to a crazy person of the wrong species. Alone in the world. At the mercy of these nutbars. Stolen from its natural habitat. Destined to serve humans. Colonized. Dispossessed. Oblivious.

It's how I feel about the cult of domesticated animals. It's wrong.

Also, I don't instantly love it like everyone else because it looks cute. Maybe I'm a psychopath. I think about stamping on it to liberate it from its disaster of a life and because I can always think of the most offensive, subversive thing to do in these situations. I text all of this to Kwe, who finds my ballet situations highly entertaining. She votes for stamping on it. "Just hunt that fucker," she types. All these people are going home to eat chicken for supper for fuck's sake, yet if I stamp on this thing, they'll call the police. *Cheep. Cheep. Cheep.*

What would I want me to do if I were the chick? Would I want me to say something smart and critical of the situation that the chick wouldn't quite get now but might turn into a light-bulb moment when she reaches adult chickenhood? I would want me as a human to save me as a chick. But how? This situation is so fucked I can't think of a way of saving that chick. Except maybe to get it away from Ivory, but I cannot in any way be responsible for this chick, because I hate it. It cheeps too much, for one thing.

The next week Ivory is not weathering the homeschooling well, and I can tell, because when you've had the biscuit, so to speak, and you've been pushed past what you can handle with kids, the tiniest thing can set off a waterfall of dysfunction. Ivory lost her car keys even though she just drove her van to ballet, and it's her husband's fault because it's always the other person's fault in these kinds of situations. She is racing around the ballet room, frantically looking everywhere. ER doctor went to her car to get a flashlight so they could look I-don't-know-where in the dark corners of the ballet waiting room. Finally, she dumps out her mega-purse onto the floor in front of me. It is a fascinating zhaaganash archeological dig of treasures. There are sandwiches in cloth ziploc-like bags, homemade granola bars, diva cups, Tibetan prayer flags, rope, chick food, tidy bun supplies, sewing stuff, an e-reader, and several other regular purse items. There is also a pair of scissors, which Ivory uses to chop her purse into strips in case the keys are in the lining.

They are not.

Three weeks later it is the recital. I'm in the dressing room with the tidy buns, feeling proud that I remembered to scrub my kid's tattoos off like the note said but now realizing I'm without a tidy bun or makeup that makes your cheeks look sunburnt or a camera or a video camera or nylon stockings that fit a six-year-old and I am not collecting things for my ballet scrapbook. Also I cannot get the costume on her. It is pink with layers of, I guess you would call it "netting," and it looks to me like cotton candy and there are four holes and I'm used to five-hole garments and I ask my kid if she is supposed to be cotton candy and she says she forgets what she is but maybe the costume is upside down. The costume is clearly broken so I text the co-parent and tell them to meet us in the back alley of the theatre after I text them a photo of the kid in her upside down cotton candy uniform so they are well aware it is an emergency situation.

They fix it because they are an artist and they understand how shit is supposed to look.

My kid is nervous. I think she should be. I am. We are in hostile tidy-bun territory without a guidebook or proper supplies or training. I lie. I tell her it's fine, she's awesome, the show will be awesome, and her costume is awesome. She tells me it doesn't feel fine and to stop saying awesome. I say that's an important feeling to pay attention to and she tells me that's not great advice at this moment. I kiss her goodbye and leave to go and find my seat in the theatre, knowing that this is the most unsafe space I've ever left my beautiful-sounding bird in, and then the curtain goes up and the show begins.

In a few minutes she comes out on stage, a brown and hoppy ball of maybe pink candy floss. It's only a few seconds before they show up, circling her close, from toes to head, weaving an invisible net of Migizi love around her as she decides she is worth more than this pointed gaze.

I'm going through your instagram feed, making a list of all your likes this month. Then I'm splitting them into four categories: bands you saw, books you read, pets & babies, and special places you went. Then I'm going to go through all the photos you posted this month and split them into the same categories. Then I'm going to go through my feed and categorize all the likes I got from you this month and use this to increase my likes from you next month. I know you love my dead animal photos because even though you're vegan or an animal rights activist or something like that you get NDNs on a fairly deep level or you don't mind dead animals or maybe you just imagine my dead animals are sleeping in NDN heaven. I know you never like my protest photos, photos of my kids doing awesome things, or my farmer's field series. I might shelve that series. I thought it was arty and you'd get it, but you're not getting it. It's not producing likes from you so I'm going to leave it this month, I think. I'm going to save these four charts in excel until the first day of next month and I'll add in my new stats. I haven't had to add a category to your chart in four months now so I'm pretty sure that your liking and posting stats have stabilized. You get the most likes from your friends for band and pet photos, and the least likes for books. Honestly you don't post very many baby pics. You don't have kids and near as I can tell you're not a baby person. But every once in a while you do post one, I think out of obligation because we just turned forty and it's everyone's last chance to procreate so we have to act excited and supportive. It's the kind thing to do.

After I'm done instagram, I'm going to go through our texts and figure out who instigated each individual texting conversation and who was the last one to reply. I personally hate being the last one to reply in a texting conversation. It's like the other person just disappears or tells you to go fuck yourself, so I try specifically now to leave most texting conversations first as a matter of principle. Except for the inner circle. Everyone who now holds membership in my inner circle always signs off a texting conversation with XO or xx or xoxo or xox or the deadly x. To get into the inner circle, in fact, you can't be a texting abandoner. That's a fucking rule.

You are no longer in my texting inner circle precisely because of these statistics. For instance, last month you instigated six texting conversations and I instigated five, but you text-abandoned me nine out of the eleven conversations. This month is different. I'm aiming for four to five abandonments at the most because I know I can quit better than you. If anything, I am the quitter in this relationship. It means that our conversations are a lot shorter and shallower but I'm not getting caught with my pants down, so to speak. Maybe I should add text-length to the chart?

Next I'm doing your fb stats. These are a lot harder to calculate, or a lot more time-consuming anyway. I stay online for the entire time you are up on Mondays so I can clock and average how much time you're on fb based on your iphone. On average, you spend four minutes per half hour of waking time on fb. You could have used those four minutes to check in on me, via text, but you didn't, so that's reason number two why you are no longer in my inner circle.

You keep quitting and then rejoining twitter, so twitter use is hard to clock. Plus I think you mostly just read people's feeds; you never participate, which isn't giving back what you are taking. Reason number three why you are no longer in my inner circle: problems with reciprocity.

If you texted me right now, I'd tell you that I'm having a dinner party. I'm having these "folks" over that use the word "folks" regularly in conversation. They are visiting his parents here on the rez and they're from the west coast so they're food snobs. Which is probably my issue. I always feel like a cheap trashy NDN when I'm on the west coast what with all the goddamn trees, mountains, ocean, and salmon, and all the goddamn white people tripping over themselves to stop pipelines. WTF. Anyway, I'm not actually that good at dinner parties. I'm good at inviting people over, drinking too much, and then collaboratively making kraft dinner well after midnight. See? That would have been a funny and uplifting texting conversation. Your loss.

I'm going to do three hundred sit-ups today because I really want a ripped abdomen and time is running out. You can't get a ripped abdomen after forty, well probably you can, but your skin is so loose you still look gross so why bother?

After I do three hundred sit-ups I'm going to the beach. I hope you text me when I am at the beach and ask me what I'm doing because I've already planned on sending you a selfie of me with my nearly ripped abdomen in a bikini. I took it last week (ok, I didn't take it. I got this dad at the beach to take it because I simply cannot take a good selfie of me on the beach), then I filtered it and photoshopped it and now it's all ready to go.

Remember that game we played when we first started texting? You would ask me, "What are you doing?" and I would have to text back immediately with whatever it was I was doing. Same went for you. Fuck. It was a great exercise really, because I got out there and did some really cool stuff in case you texted, at least at the beginning. And then I realized that if I just made a list of all the cool things I could be doing, it was more fun than actually doing all the really cool stuff. Because it felt like kind of a burn when I did something cool that I definitely wanted you to know about but then you didn't text me so you didn't get to hear about it.

I'm going on vacation next week and I have NOT decided how to handle that at all! How do I want to play it?? Do I want to pretend that I'm off the grid? Having such an incredible, fantastic, over-the-top, real-life experience that I can't possibly be dragged back down into the shallow waters of social media? Do I want people to wonder where I am? Wonder if I've logged off completely? Do I want them to miss me, and feel sad/bad about themselves? Or should I post the most outstanding four to five photos per day, maybe off my instagram feed, just amplifying the shit out of any glimmer of fun I do have? Then they'll feel bad/sad about their own lives or lack of fun and adventure, and they'll put me on a pedestal of how to really live your life to the fullest. And you. How the fuck am I going to play it with you? Remember when you went to Boston and you *almost* forgot to tell me and I would have been all, *wtf you hate me, no texts in seven days*, but it was just because you were in the States and were avoiding those deadly roaming charges but not tech-savvy enough to buy a new sim card? I sort of want you to feel like that. Like maybe I should forget to tell you I'm going and just see what happens when there are no texts from me for seven days and probably I could even go longer than seven days because for the first seven days I am going to be having some approximation of real fun in the real world so if I could go for say five more days, that would be approaching two weeks. Burn for you. The only risk is if you don't notice, which is a fairly big risk.

There is a third space. Say nothing. Post a few stellar vacation photos to fb when I know you're on your phone, and then text you the selfie with a quick "so sorry. that wasn't meant for you. soon. xo"

There is a part inside, between anatomy and physiology, that you drop breath into when you sing. If you imagine filling a balloon with air and sitting it on top of your pubic bone, the place I mean is just behind that. It controls breath but for more important reasons than the science of oxygen.

This was the part of me that was surprised when you showed up out of nowhere, wearing the same clothes as when I last saw you. This was the part of me that sped up when you got into the car like you were supposed to be there, as if it was no big deal. I wasn't even waiting. Or wondering.

It was you, and it wasn't you. It was the directive form of you, without tricky smiles and sideways glances, and that part of you that makes you fall in love with everything. It was a coded you, an algorithmic you. Now that I look back, I wonder why I wasn't suspicious, because you were all narrative.

You told me to take you to the most beautiful place in my territory.

I knew it was a test.

I knew I would pass in a way that would make you consider taking things too far. I find that interesting. I find riding the edge of taking it too far pregnant grace. People who are just learning how to walk are not afraid of taking things too far.

We know what your people think about us. We know you feel pity because the largest city in the country is on top of us, thrusting in and out like it's our benevolent Wiindigo, fucking us in time to our screams like it's death metal. Like our loss is tragic and we are small people. Like golf courses and dreamcatchers and selling out are all we have left.

You'd fight harder to keep what you have if you knew. We all would.

You and me are quiet in the car because this is what sits between us. You've come all this way so soon. You are already not satisfied with me coming into you, you want to also be in me. This is rare.

It takes forty-five minutes to get there. It's hard wall raining, making us all look depressed before noon, making my fingers and toes ache cold even though it's twenty degrees above zero. The car is singing anthems for sent runners and lost feelings. We transition from lowlands to shield. I want to impress you with this part of my land, like the Canadian Shield makes me more NDN than just deciduous trees, and then I know the pity that's draping the car isn't yours, it's mine.

I pull the car over on the muddy country road with tentative shoulders. I get out and you follow. We walk up the hill on the road whose damage time has made too deep for travelling. We take the path down to the spot where the river's body secretly drops and takes a sharp turn to the west, throwing the water into a kind of chaos you can hear and see and taste.

I'm careful not to overlay emotion onto this reality. The water isn't angry even though its strong is carving rock. It isn't even confused because of the crucial interruption in its flow. Its sound is just a rupture so other voices can be heard.

I climb over the fence and walk down the rocky bank, taking a big step out onto a ledge overhanging the canyon. The water is high, and the rocks are slippery. I pretend fearless.

I sit.
Beside.

Your lips on my forehead.
Your arms.

There is a part inside between anatomy and physiology that you drop breath into when you sing. If you imagine filling a balloon with air and sitting it on top of your pubic bone, the place I mean is just behind that. It controls breath but for more important reasons than the science of oxygen.

This is the part of me that dissolved.

You are no longer directive. Your freckles are back and your mischievous eyes are trying to catch mine and I can see your light again. I wonder who brought you here and why you came and what sorts of expectations you've brought in your backpack.

You sit up and so do I. I turn towards the falls and the wounded canyon and pull my knees towards my chest so I can rest my head on them.

I wonder what you'll try and take.

I wonder how I'll have to pay.

I drop tobacco into the water unceremoniously, like the old days.

You hand me a stick of red licorice, and we both smile.

omg. chi'miigwech for last night. you are so sweet & so fun. #crush.

i don't know what this thing between you & me is supposed to be. #love #whatarewe?! #lol

we have to play it cool. you can't be liking everything i post. be careful of that. #weweni #playitcool

you can't be never liking my posts either. for one thing that sends me into an #existentialcrisis & too few likes could mean you're mad or you've lost interest or you've moved on or you're purposely trying not to like my posts. ☹

GREAT IDEA: log on to smartberrytracker™ to keep track. it automatically gives you your totals for each ¼ hour and then averages over days & weeks. #STAY WITHIN THE TARGETS. it's the only way to meet our #relationshipgoals

i want you to know that i am always here for you and that we can talk about whatever you want. #alwayshere #4ever

i love you. #gizaagiin #anishinaabemowin ☺

i want you to know that when i said i was always here, i meant it. smartberry™ chat me if you're anxious kwe. i am well aware that we are all supposed to get 3 hours of non-screen time a week and i'm committed to that and #forestyoga because i #lovelife and smartberry™ powers down for 4 minutes every hour through the night so I'm covered. #imhere #covered #goodlife so it's been 45 minutes and i haven't heard from you and i know you are meeting with del for americanos so i'm just going to assume that you guys are good. #besties #caffeine

whatcha up to kwe? #miss #love

i can see you're on smartberry™ chat by that red dot by your name and i can see del's on smartberry™ chat because they also have that big stupid red dot by their name and you can both see that i'm on smartberry™ chat because i must also have that big stupid red dot by my name but nobody is smartberry™ chatting with me so i can only assume you are smartberry™ chatting with them which seems exactly the same as you having the same kind of sex i imagine having with you with them in front of me. #ugh #jealous ☹ ☹ ☹

i just posted a photo of me harvesting birch bark at this time last year and after 3 minutes I already have 50 smartberry™ likes and i totally feel better even though you still haven't texted. #nativer-thanyou #hollaatmekwe

you were on smartberry™ chat one minute ago and i posted that 3 minutes ago so you've seen it, and you didn't give me a like. ☹ #relationshipgoals

kwe. what's up? did you see that? i just posted the smartberry™ video of sisters so people don't think im just self promoting. #ATCR #wow #throwback #retro

i KNOW. it's 3:32 minutes long! i only watched the first 30 sec. #wtf #oldstuffissolong

glad it went good with del. i'm good. i'm just deciding which photo from the powwow to post for #throwbacktuesday #hoop or #jingle?

#notjustselfpromoting #community

totes. #hoop it is.

have you eaten?

i'm fine. i'm smartberry™ polychatting with makwa, migizi & wag-osh. they are totally coming tonight to my book launch. #excited.

kwe i don't know what to wear. #help! #fashion911 #profesh

yep i posted it. got lots of suggestions. working on it. #wardrobe #booklaunch #Airplanemode

if i don't get like 450 likes in the first minute of launching i'm going to fucking die. i WILL NOT be able to take it. #Airplanemode #tobaccodownprayersup

where are you? you HAVE to be there. #booklaunch #Airplanemode

fuk. i hope i bought enough #initiallikes™ and #initialshares™ #Airplanemode

5 mins out #Airplanemodelaunch

people better like this book. #fingerscrossed #nervous #Airplanemode

omfg. you're NOT ON smartberry™? WTF. starting in 4 minutes. #nightmare

it's fine. it's totally fine. i'm sorry too. #stressedout #fml

#remembertobreathe #centre #debwe

ONE MINUTE!!!! #AirplanemodeLaunch #Airplanemode

kwe, this is it. Airplane Mode THE BOOK is launching. so. fucking. pumped. #sopumped #Airplanemode #ndnlit #canlit #canpoli

launching . . .

Airplane Mode

I'd like to apologize to you specifically for giving you that half-assed hug the other day when I ran into you at the airport. I was uncomfortable and irritated because smartberry™ was almost out of battery even though I put it in airplane mode for most of the day and I was trying not to lose it after showing my boarding pass, and I was also trying to get my belt back on and not be accused of smuggling creatorswater™ through the security checkpoint, and then — surprise — there you were. If I'd had time to sort of, you know, smartberry™ chat you first and think this entire interaction through and be the person I want to be instead of the person I am, I would have looked you in the eye, walked into your breath, and felt the heat of your body against mine. I would have brought my arms up to your chest and then just paused so our faces could find each other, so our skin could just get used to things. You would have kissed my forehead because I'm always smartberry™ chatting about that. We would both look down, but you're taller, so you'd look down onto me. My arms would surround you and mostly we would both be glad. The End.

aww miigs. kwe. i know. i love that part too. no, no, i totally meant that. #muse #love #connection so #awesome. #whew. #Airplanemode

#635 likes in the first min! #bestseller #art #ndnlit #worthit

love. Xo

there are two thieves in this tent frame

there are two thieves in this tent frame
stealing back red bodies
savage desires
things we can't speak of

mii go aaniwi: despite everything, i am doing well

we are burning shame & guilt
with the moss & paper birch
while i'm shaking & leaking injury
hoping you won't look

mii go aaniwi: even when you are gone, i carry you

you whisper kwe on the stairs,
and i feel good, enough
you show me brown holding fragile
and i feel safe, enough

*mii go aaniwi: we are carrying the hard parts,
    but they don't weigh us down*

my old one taught me to make kindling this way
slicing off thin splints, but not all the way
my old one taught me miigwanawe
"it's always how *you* really are," he says just to me

mii go aaniwi: your empty isn't as empty as you think

we are thieves that feel better in the same room
    because of everything, we are doing well
we are thieves stealing back ourselves
    even when i am gone, you carry me
we are thieves, cradling our ruined
    we are carrying the hard parts, & they lift us up
there are two thieves in this tent frame
    your empty is never as empty as you think .

Situation Update #1

Banff is flooding in the middle of summer because it will not stop raining because of global warming and probably this is the new reality. There's a mudslide that's closed the Trans-Canada Highway. It is falling into the Delusional River. Revenge Creek is eating homes. The rescue helicopter is constantly flying overhead, taking photos near as I can tell. All the trails and roads are closed.

Situation Update #2

Doing a writing residency right now is stupid. I don't know how to manage inspiration, grant writing, and booking time off to write six months in advance. It's a fucking disaster.

Also I'm not really a writer and I don't know how I wrote those other books or why John published them or why people read them. People should know I'm a fraud. Plus residencies are for rich white people and who the fuck am I to be here. I have no business being here.

I feel like a traitor.

If Frantz Fanon walked into this architecturally designed hut at the Banff Centre for the Oil Arts he'd be so fucking disappointed in me or else he'd love me for validating *Black Skin, White Masks*. As if Fanon gives two fucks about me.

Plus there's always pressure in a residency. Like the bus from the airport is the starting block and once you have your room key the starting pistol goes off and bang.

Fuck, I can complain about anything. Really, I can't stand myself.

Plus, the flood. Write what you know. And it's a flood.

Situation Update #3

I'm reading Settler Colonial's twitter feed because he doesn't miss anything, and so of course he's tweeting exactly what racist

Canadians tweet when one of our rez's gets flooded — relocate Calgary.

The conditions during this flood are still 90 percent better than conditions on many reserves.

Honestly, I enjoy white people's mega-tar-sands-industry homes getting sucked into the river. I do. It just seems fair.

Situation Update #4

There are a lot of natural-disaster tourists here who have never been happier. They are going from one area of the town to the other, taking instagram photos of high water. So am I.

I just googled the water treatment facility in Banff and learned that it is high on Tunnel Mountain. That's good. We'll have drinking water! Or we could just open our mouths and tilt them up.

Floods are mostly great, except for that Bible one and that Nanabush one. People don't often get hurt. They are naturally occurring events. They remind us of the power of the land and the power of water. But the reminder never sticks. David Suzuki is trying to rightly connect this event to climate change, because of course that's true, but really Canadians don't give a shit. I like how hard he tries though.

Situation Update #5

One person has texted me to see if I am ok. One.

Situation Update #6

Maybe I should text people I know that are in Calgary and see if they are ok.

Is that too forward? Too boundary-pressing? Breaking the texting boundary? What if they cringe when they get my text and are all like, FUCK it's a white-collar disaster.

Kindness is a goddamn art.

Situation Update #7

I met my partner during the flood of the century in 1997 in Winnipeg. I know. Super romantic. We actually met at a bar and we were kinda drunk. But whatever. The flood was on and so were we.

So this flood reminds me of that flood, but there are key differences. Winnipeg, you know how to sandbag. There are stations, there are hundreds of volunteers, the bagging of the sand takes place in the same place as the sandbags are needed, and people know how to architect sandbags into amazing triangular walls of steel.

Here, it's different. There is one sandbag-filling station at the dog park. There are eight people there but they don't want more volunteers. People are loading their fifteen sandbags into the trunk of their car and laying them on their lawns with big spaces in between them.

It's driving my partner insane. He keeps yelling: "THESE PEOPLE DON'T KNOW HOW TO SANDBAG. THESE PEOPLE DON'T KNOW WHAT TO DO IN THE EVENT OF A FLOOD. YOU FUCK UP A FLOOD IN WINNIPEG, YOU NEVER GET ELECTED AGAIN."

Situation Update #8

Sled Island Music Festival is cancelled. It seems like they were real troupers at the beginning of the flood, sticking performers in movie theatres, but now the entire downtown core of Calgary is evacuated, including them, so it's all over.

No Jesus and Mary Chain for Calgary.

I was Jesus and Mary Chain's biggest fan in grade ten. I did an english project on their lyrics, and if you read their lyrics, that, my friend, is no easy task.

Also, the zoo is evacuated. Everyone has been asking: What about the zoo! It's on an island! I've hoped to never have to endure the Calgary Zoo, so it wasn't a question I was asking. The big cats have been moved to the courthouse jail cells. Metaphors melt away during floods.

Situation Update #9

I'm reading another writer's twitter feed because he is trapped in Canmore and writing for the *national post*. That fucker. Making money off this tragedy we're stuck in. Except Naomi says that is what natural disasters are for when we're trapped in capitalism. He seems frantic. It's worse over there, though. Like they could run out of coffee. And actually monster homes have fallen into the river and there's water on the first floor of his hotel.

Situation Update #10

This flood is really just inconvenient. It's like being trapped in a natural-disaster theme park.

It's also my fourth flood of the century and I'm not even half a century old.

There is something about these kinds of natural disasters that makes my mind always try to think of the smartest response. So I imagine that I'm the one that stockpiled the particular item — toilet paper, gas, bottled water, matches — that everyone suddenly needs. That I'm the one that thought ahead and was prepared. This fantasy is always tempered by a desire to not be the one that's living in a bomb shelter with six thousand cans of tomato soup. I can't imagine myself selling toilet paper to some desperate rich white person for twenty-five dollars. I'd probably just give away all my stockpiled stuff, revelling in how "just in case" finally fucking paid off.

Situation Update #11

You're supposed to stay away from the river. It isn't even a river anymore. In some places it's a full-fledged lake and other places it's a waterfall, only the water doesn't drop so the fall doesn't stop, it just continues. It's that angry.

Well, the river isn't angry at all. It's just doing what it does when three hundred millimetres of rain falls into it during spring run-off.

It looks like chocolate milk. Some old guy that's lived here for thirty years and drives a bus to Vancouver for Brewster says that when the snow melts into the mountains the river is like a coffee with too much milk for one week. That's what we're seeing.

I crossed the police tape with all the other tourists to see Bow Falls. It isn't a falls anymore at all. It just looks like the rest of the river.

Situation Update #12
Safeway looks like it has been ransacked. There is no bottled water and no toilet paper. I make a mental note that in a disaster situation those are the two things to buy up in great quantity, even though only one of them is essential.

No one has ever died from a lack of toilet paper.

Also we are running out of gas. But that's ok, because there is no place to go, because all the roads are closed.

Apparently gas trucks and food trucks from Calgary are going to come once the mudslide gets cleaned up. They are going to route them through Fernie.

Situation Update #13
Aboriginal Day at the Banff Centre has been cancelled due to the emergency situation and the weather. CANCELLED.

Thank fucking god. I was dreading us being the only NDNs in the crowd of eight hundred white people. It was going to be humiliating, but I was going to put on a brave face for the kids.

Situation Update #14
I am imagining myself being interviewed by CBC on the "Aboriginal" perspective of the flood. First I imagine the interviewer trying to lead me into saying shit like, "Mother Earth is so powerful. The water is so sacred. White people shouldn't build their houses upon the sand."

Then I imagine myself getting all aggressive and trying to get them to see the double standard in reporting flooding in Calgary and not reporting flooding in say Attawapiskat.

But they never get that. Because it's inconvenient for them we're not dead.

The whole scenario doesn't even make sense, because the CBC only wants our opinions on corrupt chiefs, child poverty, and conflict within the AFN.

Situation Update #15
Jonathan Goldstein is in cabin number four. I tried to brag that around a bit with my friends but nobody knew who he was.

Then I bought the cheaper e-version of his book *I'll Seize the Day Tomorrow*, in case I run into him on the path. Then I could say, "Hey. I read your book. You're the *WireTap* guy."

Then I listen to a bunch of *This American Life* episodes. Then I go to *DNTO* and listen to all those stories. Why don't I write for them? Well, because I have a fair amount of contempt for all the middle-class white people huddled around their radios listening to that shit. That's why.

Then I read his twitter feed. He's tweeting about being in the bush in his underwear drinking dimetapp. I watch for actual evidence of that. I believe writers should do the shit they write about. Also I wonder if safeway is out of dimetapp yet.

Situation Update #16
I think I actually hate writing because I hate sitting on chairs.

Situation Update #17
I just heard a bird sing because it finally stopped raining. If you look up, though, we've probably only got about ten minutes.

Situation Update #18
You'd think the Christians would be building a big ark. It saved the world the first time, according to them, so really, if churches had

arks all ready to go, "just in case," then that could be a real help in situations like these. HEAD TO THE ARK IMMEDIATELY. HEAD TO THE ARK IMMEDIATELY. Plus you could bring your pets and for sure they would make a separate compartment for NDNs and race traitors. But woah, woah, don't get all liberal on me, the separate compartment is perfect. No one wants to be stuck on a goddamn ark with a bunch of extra-self-righteous Christians because they called it, you know, with the ark. Again.

The Nishnaabe, though, we didn't waste time building an ark. Because why? In a flood there are, like, trees everywhere and what's funner than riding the rapids on a log, and why not live in the moment instead of living inside just in case.

That's right, Dad, I just used the word "funner."

My god, I wonder what artist cabin number two is doing. I think she's an old white poet. But her artist cabin is a BOAT and she's in a flood. I bet her process is fucked right now.

Situation Update #19
Situation update #12 from the Town of Banff just came in and holy shit that fucking other writer has another column.

The gist of the update is this: All the roads are still closed. You can leave going west, but there is a high chance of mudslides so you can't be guaranteed to get back. You're never going to get to Calgary again. It says some other things, but nobody proofread it so it's hard to understand. STAY AWAY FROM THE RIVER.

There is a guest book in the artist hut where people write sappy things about how amazing and productive and inspiring their residency was. I hate guest books. I'm thinking about writing "You are on Blackfoot land" on the next ten pages of the book, forcing people to flip through it before they can add all their gratitude. Gratitude is so contrived.

Situation Update #20

I want to be the kind of person that is good at making the best of a bad situation. We're not in a bad situation, but still, it's good practice, because I'm not actually a person that is good at making the best of a bad situation. What I am good at is satire and sarcasm, which I tend to use to make good situations bad. How hard could it be to make things go the opposite way?

I start by stating all the great things about this very moment. The sun is sort of trying to come out. The bird I heard a few pages ago is back. But it's feeling forced because it's not actually how I feel. Most of the time I think I actually feel nothing. Or I feel anxiety. It's pretty rare to have a good feeling. It needs to be a pretty overwhelming good thing that's happened for me to have a good feeling and even then I can't maintain it that long. Good feelings are fleeting.

I'd like to find out if this is normal. It seems like perpetually happy people live in some sort of state of denial, constantly orgasming into the next moment, and happy people rarely do anything I think is important. Mostly they are annoying. Well, happy people do make great parents. I think that's true. Sometimes it isn't annoying to be around happy people. Sometimes it is possible to get swept up in whatever denial they have going on.

Situation Update #21

Uh oh. THE OTHER WRITER is a retweeter of compliments. May have to unfollow.

Situation Update #22

Getting old sucks. If you talk to old people, really old people and regular old people, they will tell you: aging is a painful betrayal of the body and the mind. So I'm thinking that one needs a plan. I'm wondering if old people think of this — that really, past age seventy-five is the time for smoking, drinking, and drugs. You're going to die soon anyway so the health warnings don't apply. Plus I can imagine there is a lot of anxiety in being close to death. Smoking and drinking manages that anxiety. Plus all your friends are dead or dying and you've always embarrassed your kids no matter what you did anyway so why not. It's an untapped market.

I know we like to think that by seventy-five we'll have everything all figured out and be happy and at peace. But that's not true for twenty, thirty, or forty, so why would it be true for seventy?

Situation Update #23

Watching what's happening in Calgary on TV. Tons of help. Watching on twitter and fb what's happening in First Nation communities like Morley. Nothing. No help. Help would be a federal responsibility and the feds spent all the money on litigating against First Nations and on surveillance.

Situation Update #24

I think that what I am writing is stupid, but there's no capacity here to write about anything else. Last night the power went out. First there were rumours that a transformer exploded and the RCMP was involved, but then it turns out they were just trying to divert water away from the transformer, and it got wet and blew up. Immediately, authorities put out an extreme water conservation alert on twitter; so extreme, they asked people to call their non-twitter friends to inform them not to wash anything or take showers. This alerted me to the fact that when the power goes out in Banff, they can't process water. There is also no water tower.

So I got competitive and stockpiled water in all available containers. I tried to wake my partner up but he didn't care. He didn't even read the status update. In the morning, he seems sure he can filter water from the Delusional River with a handful of sand and saran wrap and some coffee filters. While he's doing that, I'll just put a bucket outside.

Situation Update #25

It's stopped raining and I'm feeling a LOT less Biblical. Stopping raining is the first step to stopping flooding. That means the situation should be returning to normal and I should be returning to normal writing, even though only one day is left in my residency, and to celebrate, the head of the Banff Centre is having a free cocktail party for all the people that have survived thus far, which for sure means free sparkly water.

Status Update #26

The road is open in one direction and we have the entire national park to ourselves. A gift no NDN should waste.

ACKNOWLEDGEMENTS

"Airplane Mode" was previously published in *Kimiwan 'Zine*, issue 8, fall 2014; "Selfie" was published in *As/Us* literary journal, issue 4, fall 2014; "Leaning In" was published by the Art Gallery of Windsor and again in *Decolonization, Indigeneity, Education and Society* volume 3, issue 1, fall 2014; "Seeing Through the End of the World" was published in *Kimiwan 'Zine,* issue 6, 2014; "Akiden Boreal" was published by House of Anansi press in an ebook as part of Luminato's *The North-South Project*, 2015; "constellation" was published by *C Magazine*, fall 2015; "i am graffiti" was published in *The Walrus*, summer 2015; "how to steal a canoe" won an Editors' Choice Award in *Arc Poetry Magazine*'s Poem of the Year contest and was published in *Arc Poetry Magazine* 77, spring 2015; "caribou ghosts & untold stories" and "this accident of being lost" were published in *Arc Poetry Magazine* 76, winter 2015. This work was financially supported by the Ontario Arts Council. Thanks to the team at House of Anansi Press, especially Janie, for their ongoing support of this work.

Chi'miigwech to Rebecca Belmore for the cover image, and for the revolution her work invokes in me.

I am forever grateful to my editor, Damian Rogers, for caring so deeply about these stories and for holding space for me in the literary world. Damian went beyond the standard job of the editor in her acknowledgement that these stories were born out of a Nishnaabeg world. She followed me to uncomfortable places, listened very deeply, advocated for me, and encouraged me to pursue artistic excellence according to my nation's storytelling practices. She supported my desire to write these stories unapologetically and truthfully so I see myself and my community in these pages. She protected the part of me that can create and respected my sovereignty throughout this process, and for that I'm eternally grateful.

I AM GRAFFITI The lines "three white Xs / on the wall of the grocery store" reference the performance piece *X* by artist Rebecca Belmore.

PLIGHT, DOING THE RIGHT THING The character Sabe is a Bagwajiwininiwag within the context of the Nishnaabeg, known in english as Bigfoot.

CARIBOU GHOSTS & UNTOLD STORIES The line "train tracks six pack riff raff" was posted by the Vancouver-based slam poet Zaccheus Jackson on instagram hours before he died in Toronto. The phrase "best trained troops that refuse to fight" is based on the beginning sample from Public Enemy's song "Fight the Power," from a speech by civil rights attorney and activist Thomas "TNT" Todd in which he used the line "our best-trained...troops refuse to fight."

CONSTELLATION The line "mama = your first ocean" is based on a line from the poem "52 Notes for the Products of Conception" by Damian Rogers, which appears in her collection *Dear Leader* (Coach House, 2015). Used with permission.

TRAVEL TO ME NOW An adapted version of this piece is part of a track of the same name on Tara Williamson's 2016 record *Songs to Keep Us Warm*. The line "there's nothing in this that isn't love" riffs on a line from the poem "You Cannot Shed the Difficult, Most Stubborn Aspects of Your Nature with One Dose" by Damian Rogers, which appears in her collection *Dear Leader*. Used with permission.

LEANING IN Ashkiwiwininiwag, according to Elder Doug Williams, were Mississauga Nishnaabeg guerilla fighters that were so-named because they surprised their foe as if they were jumping out of piles of leaves; *Zhaawanoog* (Zhauwunook) literally means "the people of the south" and is the Anishinaabe name for the Shawnee, according to Basil Johnston in his *Anishinaubae Thesaurus*; *Tkamse* and *Taagaamose* are Anishinaabeg names, each from a different dialect, with the same meaning as the Shawnee *Tecumseh*. *Taagaamose* comes from Dr. Tobasonakwutiban Kinew and is used with the permission of his son, Wab Kinew. I learned the word *Tkamse* and its meaning from Anishinaabe scholar Brock Pitawanakwat. *Bizhiw gidoodem* means "lynx is your clan." *Eniigaanizijig* means "leader." *Deshkaan Ziibing* means "antler river" and is the Anishinaabe name for the Thames River, along which Tecumseh died. I learned this word from Eva Jewell. *Binaakwe Giizis* is October. Zhaawan (South) and Niibin (Summer) are two spirits in Anishinaabeg thought. Bkejwanong is Wapole Island.

ROAD SALT The line "hostages first trap themselves" is from Lee Maracle's *Celia's Song* (Cormorant Books, 2014), and is used with permission.

MINOMIINIKESHII SINGS The line "long rays of deepening sun" is from Louise Erdrich's *Books and Islands in Ojibwe Country*, and I learned about Minomiinikeshi, the spirit of wild rice, first from this source. "If the stalk is floppy, we call it a poor erection" and "if the stalk is too wet, we call it a penis soaking in its favorite place" are direct translations of Anishinaabeg words from Kathi Avery Kinew's Ph.D. dissertation at the University of Manitoba, called "Manito Gitigaan, Governing in the Great Spirit's Garden: Wild Rice in Treaty #3." The idea of "before it's illegal to be together" also . comes from Kinew's work. Both of these works carry the knowledge of Tobasonakwutiban Kinew.

UNSUBSTANTIATED HEALTH BENEFITS The line "I'm lost, I'm afraid. A frayed rope tying down a leaky boat to the roof of a car on the road in the dark and it's snowing" is from the song "Reconstruction Site" by the Weakerthans, written by John K. Samson, and is used with permission.

PRETENDING FEARLESS This story references the line "Someone send a runner / through the weather that I'm under / for the feeling that I lost today" from the song "England" by the National, which appears on their record *High Violet*.

©Nadya Kwandibens

LEANNE BETASAMOSAKE SIMPSON is a Michi Saagiig Nishnaabeg writer, scholar, and musician, and is a member of Alderville First Nation. She holds a Ph.D. from the University of Manitoba and has lectured at universities across Canada. She is the author of six books, including *Islands of Decolonial Love*, and the editor of three anthologies. She has released two albums, including *f(l)ight*, which is a companion piece to this collection.